DREAM OF SHADOWS

Issue 2

Dream of Shadows Issue 2 © June 2020, Independently Published

ISBN: 9798663242851

Cover: Blue Burning Wraith © Austin Gragg, 2020
The Wee Small Hours © Travis Burnham, 2020
On the Inside © John A. McColley, 2020
An Island, Surrounded by a Sea of Death © Andrew Barron, 2020
Local Hero © Rajiv Moté, 2020
Weeds and Seeds © Mariah Montoya, 2020
Castrati © Bryan Miller, 2020
Moonlit Proposal © Jen Sexton-Riley, 2020
Time and Tide © Chrissie Rohrman, 2020
The Oven in the Woods © Alexander Langer, 2020
Forgive the Adoring Beast © Hailey Piper, 2020
Coyote-Faced Woman © Marissa James, 2020
The Portrait in the Pines © Kurt Newton, 2020
Time After Time © Morgan Elektra, 2020
Enlightenment Adrift © Steven Rooke, 2020

All rights reserved. No part of this publication may be reproduced in any form by any means, electronic, mechanical, photocopying, recording or otherwise, without prior written permission of the copyright holder.

CONTENTS

THE WEE SMALL HOURS..................................5
ON THE INSIDE..13
AN ISLAND, SURROUNDED BY A SEA OF DEATH..19
LOCAL HERO...27
WEEDS AND SEEDS...33
CASTRATI...39
MOONLIT PROPOSAL..43
TIME AND TIDE...47
THE OVEN IN THE WOODS..............................53
FORGIVE THE ADORING BEAST....................59
COYOTE-FACED WOMAN...............................65
THE PORTRAIT IN THE PINES........................71
TIME AFTER TIME...79
BONUS STORY: ENLIGHTENMENT ADRIFT..87
ABOUT THE AUTHORS....................................115

THE WEE SMALL HOURS

by
Travis Burnham

I'm sitting at the top of the cellar stairs in my son Connor's abandoned house, shotgun across my lap, trying to atone for a host of sins. Besides the 12-gauge, my son's dog, Hal 9000, and two thermoses of coffee are my only companions.

Along the cellar door's frame are long gouged furrows and dark stains. I've kept Connor's place up but have never liked to stay long or think about what those stains mean. I look after Hal, too. He's a pit bull terrier rescue and all heart.

My name's Jessup, and after thirty-eight years of drink, I'm one year sober. Before I was straight, I made just about every mistake, parenting and otherwise, that one could make. Too much time trucking, bundled out on the big road crossing from Bikini to Beantown to the Left Coast, and the time at home lost in an alcohol haze.

It was a year ago today that my son and his wife disappeared. He'd said, "There's something in our house coming to kill Jenny and me."

He rambled on about some book he'd been reading that he'd found nailed to a cellar support beam with a rusty railroad spike. The book had been written in Old Irish, a language he had no business being able to read. He'd said *they* came once a year at the winter solstice and there was no escaping them.

I put Sinatra's 'The Wee Small Hours' on the record player, and Frank began crooning about loneliness and lost love. It was whistling in the graveyard, but Frank was doing it for me. The dark hours were always the toughest for me, when my regrets came knocking at my doors and I started getting a thirst to forget those regrets.

I'm not one for believing crazy, but it was more believable than the alternative: police said that Connor had murdered Jenny, which was unimaginable – he loved Jenny like radials love the interstate. They never found her body, just enough blood to suggest she hadn't survived the loss. Connor was never found. On the lam, they said.

Hal was here at the house that night, out in the backyard. Broke four claws and chipped a tooth trying to get in. Barked himself hoarse, and his vocal cords never recovered. I have a thousand times more respect for him than I do the cops – he at least tried. He's been my rock ever since.

So if Connor's *they* came once a year, then Hal and I will be waiting right here for them. I hadn't been a good dad. Least I could do was clear Connor's name.

I took a sip of coffee as midnight came and

went without leaving a forwarding address.

Some minutes later, a low thrum ran through the house, probably a big truck going by on 95th street, a Come-a-part B series engine, judging from the rattle. Cats fought somewhere off in the distance, howling like demons. Then something upstairs fell and broke.

Slow and calm, I eased up the stairs, shotgun in the lead, Hal at my side.

Searching, I finally found a pile of broken glass on the bathroom floor, a broken frame and picture resting in the wreckage. The picture was Connor and Jenny on their honeymoon, grinning like fools with tropical drinks, beach and ocean in the background.

Jenny was good for him, kept him on his meds. She was an angel, that one. That same year, Connor had gotten his company up and running, making websites or something.

I'd never told him how proud I was of him. Not even sure I ever told him I loved him.

I glanced in the mirror, and Connor was looking out at me. It punched the breath out of my chest. He looked deformed, hunched and feral. I blinked and he was gone.

Coffee jitters. One coffee thermos was a dead soldier, but the other was safe from me. No more go-go juice.

Ever since sophomore year of college, Connor had had some troubles with hearing voices that weren't there. Doctor's had some fancy words for what ailed him, but I didn't put much stock in that, thought he'd maybe just lost touch a little bit. I'd had days like that. His mom, too. Still, I'd been drunk and had only in hindsight seen how earnest my son had been.

The next day, he and Jenny were gone.

I failed Connor when he was a kid, because Budweiser and Johnny Walker sure as hell hadn't raised him, and I failed him again when he asked for help and I wrote it off.

When 12:15 am came, I heard some scraping and scratching in the walls.

Rats? Hal didn't bark, just watched the wall with his eyes, but the noise put my nerves on edge. I turned the Sinatra up. As the night ground on, the decision to quit the sauce a year ago seemed like a terrible idea.

The noises wouldn't quit, got louder even when I pounded on the walls, so I grabbed a boning knife from the kitchen and rammed it through the sheetrock, aiming for the noises. Hal barked this time, but it almost seemed like he was barking at me.

I rammed the knife home again and again, high and low, until finally, I got something.

The thing pinned and thrashed against the blade. Blood spilled out from the wounded wall, a lot more blood than a rat holds.

A weak, muffled moan from inside the wall asked, "Why?"

I yanked the knife out. I knew the voice. My

knees went liquid. Hal whimpered.

I splayed my hand against the wall. "Jenny?"

There was a slithering from the bottom of the wall as something slipped away.

The frame of the entire house groaned, a low and deep grumbling that started in the cellar and worked its way up through the bones of the house, setting my shattered nerves even more on edge.

Feeling weak, I dropped back in my chair near the cellar door, my fingers flexing, keenly feeling the smooth, cool absence of a whisky tumbler.

The stairs creaked, and then again, as something ascended from the thick, black dark.

I leveled both shotgun barrels at the landing of the stairs.

Someone stepped up. Curly black hair run through with gray. The stench of decay washed out of the doorway. Then with another step, a face came into view. My green eyes.

"Dad." The voice was gravelly and full of broken glass.

There was a slow echo to his voice, as if there were other people whispering the same word in the background. The faint trace of Jenny's voice spoke among the quiet cacophony.

"Connor," I replied.

Something got in my eye, and I ran the cuff of my sleeve across my face to clear it. Hal gave a low whine in the back of his throat.

"Jenny and I are with them now," Connor said.

Even greater than my terror, it broke my heart thinking of them alone with these things.

He took another step up and closer.

His skin was putrid and swollen. His left arm was a mass of tentacles, his right gnarled and clawed. Things writhed beneath the fabric of his clothes, the last set I'd seen him wearing.

Using the shotgun as a cane, I levered myself to my feet. I raised the shotgun, cursing my treacherous, shaking hands. My breathing was fast, labored. I swallowed, hard.

Connor held out his hand. "Hey, Mr. 9000." His nickname for Hal.

Hal moved forward before I could grab his collar. He sniffed Connor's gnarled hand, wagged his tail. Didn't dogs have advanced senses? Was Hal seeing something that I wasn't?

The tentacles slithered around Hal, and then into him. Pushing into his eye sockets, burrowing into his ears. And then he was gone, pulled into the shadows, absorbed with not even a whimper.

I wasn't ready for that. I screamed and fired two shells into the ceiling. Plaster sprayed everywhere. I wanted to shoot Connor, shoot myself.

"Join us, Dad."

I wouldn't fail Connor again. I'd only believed in booze and myself before, but that had just left me lonely and broken.

I grit me teeth. "I love you, Connor."

I threw down the shotgun, yelling as I charged forward to embrace my son and rejoin my family.

The razored tentacles slipped beneath my skin and wound their way through my veins. Talons slid into the back of my skull and my vision burned white as sweet, hot pain exploded through my body.

That, and a deep sense of belonging throbbed through me, echoing with every pulse.

Yes. I'd never leave my family again.

ON THE INSIDE

by
John A. McColley

Lights stab through the night between dry leaves and branches slapping our face as we scramble on three legs. It's not the way these things usually walk. It's awkward, but one of our lower legs is damaged and we're being chased.

My stupid prey had a knife, screamed before I could slide off this corpse. It's losing its cohesion as well as its flavor. If I don't find another one in a few hours, I'll be forced to slorp around in the shadows, hoping to find a sleeping creature to invade. Who knows where my next ride, my next meal, will come from?

It best come soon. This one's bones are crumbling. Its muscles are fraying like cheap twine. The skin is more long, jagged holes than cohesive bag. I'm doing all the work holding organs and fluids in, and it's not making me the least bit happy.

The hole in our leg doesn't bother me so much, the nerves have been cold for a while. I shut them down as soon as I took hold, as I learned centuries ago in France. Transferring unnoticed can be better than fighting sometimes – simple, easy, quiet. Tenderizing is overrated for meals on the hoof. Or foot, I guess, in this case.

Most of us hunt, making a show of the capture. The scent of fear, the adrenaline as we settle into the skin, they add a special something to the joining. We can blend in, be less noticed, shifting our colors like our sea-dwelling kin, the cephalopods. Normally, we're ghostly white.

Did you ever wonder why clowns are white with exaggerated features? It's because in the beginning, we were clumsy. We took someone, they'd flail around, tumbling about and knocking things down. We would try to hide, make face markings as we tried to control our prey, but the results were pretty grotesque.

At the circus, I color around the mouth, triangles by the eyes, spots on the cheeks. It's like an homage to my ancestors. A baggy costume and a wig and none's the wiser.

Warning tales turned to history and faded to a joke that's always been there. But some of you remember, deep in your hind brains, and fear us, too. You never knew why you were afraid of clowns, did you? Well, there it is. You're our prey. They're what we look like when we consume you.

The leg wound bleeds, filling our shoe around long toes, seeping out and leaving a trail. Dogs howl, whine at something they don't quite recognize. Still, they pull at their chains, the urge to follow blood overwhelming. I know that feeling.

I've got to find a place to hide or a human to

ride.

The smells of damp leaves and mold fill our nostrils, the host sending me the signals. The air is cooler than I expected for Tennessee in late September and carries a thread of smoke.

Where's smoke, there's prey.

Music and laughter drift along, intensifying as the smoke does. We stumble up behind a tree, peering around into a campfire. Up the hill, light streams through narrow trees. A building. So close. We can't have made it two miles from the circus tents, but I'm in dire need. There's no time to be choosy or put more distance between me and the prey turned hunters.

"I've gotta raise the water level. I'll be right back," says a young male.

"Aww, Marv, can't you just go up to the Stuffmart? I have to swim in that river," a young female complains.

Marv doesn't respond, but heads right for me.

I scramble up the tree, catching one of the balloon-like legs of my outfit on a branch. I pull, pull again until something tears and the only thing keeping the leg on the body is me, stretched thin and exposed, catching firelight.

Marv screams.

I pull away from the leg, letting it drop right in front of him.

"What is it, Marv? Leave your thing at home? Or just can't find it?" Another male youth calls.

"Fuck you, Al–"

15

I drop. There's no time to waste. This body is falling apart by the second now, the other front leg liquefying under our grip on the tree branch. I let the rest of the body drop away, this time flinging it behind Marv. He looks up as I fall, flow over his mouth, quelling calls for help. I take a shortcut through the ear and grip his simple brain. It's awash in alcohol and other chemicals I don't recognize, but also fear...

I turn my new body around.

"Nothin'. Just about pissed on a raccoon. Headin' up to the store after all," I say, keeping the vocal chords loose, panic free, even though I haven't fully taken over yet.

Ol' Marv is still conscious. It's a risk talking, being caught, but I have to get the body away.

"If you're goin' up there, bring us back some more chips and hot dogs," one of the others calls behind us. I can't spare enough attention to tell whether it's the male or female.

We let out a grunt of assent and keep moving upward.

I don't like the bright lights of the parking lot, but if we can get a car, getting back to the circus will be easy. A bit of coloration change and the humans will never know what happened to 'Slappikins'. Clowns come and go all the time. Signing up with a new face, new name, will be easy.

This thing has some kind of sludge in its mouth. I spit it out. It's brown and appears to be some kind of plant matter. The stream of saliva smells horrible as it hangs briefly from the lower lip.

"What's going on?" Marv asks inside our head.

We stand just off the tarmac. It's fresh and smells terrible, tickling our nose. What is it with this planet and its wide array of stenches?

"We're going for a little ride. Didn't you ever want to run away to the circus when you were little?"

"Not really."

"Too bad, not that it'll make much difference. I only need enough of you to drive one of these home. I never did bother to learn. Why should I when you are such good chauffeurs?"

"I'm not driving you any–"

"Annnnd sleep," I cut him off.

Humans may be good eating, mobile, plentiful, but they're not the best conversationalists.

It only takes another minute to find a car with a window cracked open. One tendril still insinuated in Marv's brain, I slide down our arm and reach through the gap, pulling up the pin to unlock the door.

Marv convulses. I race back up his arm, but his other arm comes across. Another pellet of brown oozes out between his lips and splatters on the ground. As I watch, the hand grips me, pulling my lifeline free as Marv's mouth opens unnaturally wide.

"Sorry, pal. Ocupado," a breathy voice says. A tiny yellow eye shows at the back of Marv's throat. "Find your own ride."

"Whaaaat?" is the only word surfacing through the tumult of emotions, prime amongst them panic. "Who?"

I scan around for other prey even as I arc through the air, flung by Marv, or Marv's driver, whatever that was. The store! Halloween costumes.

"Frigging clowns," Marv says, shuddering.

I slide under a door with a poster featuring a number of smiling humans proclaiming, "We're all the same on the inside."

Filthy lies.

AN ISLAND, SURROUNDED BY A SEA OF DEATH

by
Andrew Barron

My parents were so excited when I was accepted at New Horizons. My dad initially described it as a "hippie dippy new-age school for screw-ups". That is, until his daughter turned into one of those screw-ups. Then he did a little research and found out that some people simply learned differently than others. That was me, his hippie dippy daughter.

New Horizons was just a small school in an old, abandoned and retrofitted municipal building basically in the middle of nowhere, a refuge located between the mall and the big traditional school.

But I loved it.

I loved how small the school was. About 90 students, give or take, from grades 4 through 8. No set classes or schedules to speak of. The parents, teachers and students just worked together to ensure all the curriculum standards were met. Parents were invited to drop by whenever they liked, to sit in on classes as they saw fit.

But now, all our parents and teachers are dead. At least, we're assuming they're dead because no one's tried to come get us in a couple weeks. And most of us aren't willing to consider the alternative, because if our parents aren't dead and simply left us here to die, then I don't think we could handle it.

We're stranded on an island, surrounded by a sea of death.

The worst part was that we didn't really know what was going on. Everything happened so fast. There was bits of information that found its way to us, sometimes mere words through text messages and social media posts. Words like "epidemic", "virus", "dead", "reanimated" and, eventually, "zombies".

But then the news stopped just as fast as it started. Wireless service ceased altogether almost immediately, but during that first day, there were so many calls and texts being sent that virtually nothing was going through. We're keeping our phones charged, just in case, and every once in a while, a stray, dismembered message finds its way through the ether. These messages prove to be nothing more than a gut-punch reminder of a world that no longer exists.

The TVs in our school show test patterns or static on every station. The Emergency Broadcast System didn't even broadcast for a single second. We managed to find an old radio buried in the basement, but every station simply re-plays the same bare-bones instructions on a loop. A very authoritative voice convincingly says, "Stay where you are, help is on the way.

WE WILL FIND YOU."

Stupidly, we believed the voice at first.

That message has been playing for about three weeks now. Our hope that help is, in fact, on the way is growing weaker by the day. The younger kids, when they aren't crying, hold fast to that bygone concept – hope. The most fervent and wide-eyed kids just keep repeating some variation of "mommy and daddy are coming", even though there's been no contact whatsoever from the outside world for weeks.

We're surely on borrowed time in terms of having electricity. Any day now, we'll be in darkness and silence. The lights will go out, the TVs and radio will turn off, our phones will fade for good and we'll be honestly, truly alone.

We're still trying to figure out why the dead continue to gather outside our fence. Working on theories at least gives us something to do. What buried piece of knowledge, what kernel of remembrance has sent them here? Maybe a scientist will figure that out in the future. If there's a future.

Thank God for that old fence around the perimeter, though. It was set to be removed during the next summer break, and it's nothing short of a miracle that it's withstood the incessant crush of humanity.

During the first couple of weeks, a few parents tried to drive through the sea of bodies, but they didn't make it very far. Most of the small cars chosen for the job – Civics, Corollas and other small family sedans – didn't quite have the horsepower to drive through or over a few feet of flesh, bone and blood.

If I wasn't living through the wrong end of this living nightmare, it might be slightly entertaining to watch a sick, macabre version of bowling with human pins and car balls.

Eventually, the parents graduated to using bigger cars like minivans, soccer mom SUVs and pickups with sports equipment still in the truck bed. Those provided a bit of an improvement, but they all eventually stalled out on the bodies and piles of offal underneath. Most of the drivers tried to run once their cars became stuck, but they were quickly enveloped and joined the horde, making the crowd bigger by one. Some decided to stay in their cars. What were they waiting for? A few died of starvation, but most made a run for it after a few days without food or water. The zombies didn't get much of a meal out of them.

One enterprising parent tracked down a huge Hummer – a bright yellow monster with huge tires and gleaming, spinning rims. The vanity license was DSTRYR.

I think, once I saw that truck on the hill out front was the last time I felt anything approaching optimism. It stood in the sun like a superhero, waiting to drive up to the front door and take us away from this living hellscape. The driver backed up, got a running start and plowed through. We thought they were going to make it.

We had so much hope.

But then the Hummer got tripped up after inadvertently steering directly into a fence pole. We watched in horror as the truck sat helplessly with one end of the fence pole firmly wedged into its undercarriage, the other end driven two feet into the grass, keeping the left rear tire off the ground completely while the right was kept aloft by a mound of still-moving bodies. Despite being 4-wheel drive, that Hummer wasn't going anywhere. It's a good thing the truck didn't make it past the fence, though, because it's acting as a stanch in the hole it created.

That driver didn't get out. One of my fellow students found a pair of binoculars and took a look through the windshield after a few days. He hasn't said much of anything since. The binoculars are sitting untouched on the roof where he dropped them.

When the news of the outbreak started to leak, the teachers had an impromptu "all-hands" meeting. No one truly knows what happened in that teachers' lounge, but soon after the door was closed and locked, the room was filled with screams and breaking glass, followed by silence and, then, a disturbingly steady trickle of blood from under the door.

That blood has long since dried, but no one

goes near that room anymore. The last kids to walk by it heard a light shuffling and low groaning noises.

I like to think that, despite the panic the teachers surely felt, they never opened the door, as a final act of heroism. It makes me feel a little better for some reason.

As a result, the only adult left among us kids was the janitor – Hank. He was a nice enough guy, quiet, unassuming and always willing to help, but it was a known secret throughout the school that he was an alcoholic. There was always a sour smell to him, and the outline of a handle of whiskey in the back pocket of his baggy coveralls was his trademark.

Hank stuck around for about two weeks, or roughly 72 hours after his booze ran out. Three days of withdrawal and no source of alcohol on the horizon was enough to convince him to climb the stairs to the roof where he jumped headfirst to his death without a word or a moment's hesitation.

Now Hank's doing laps around the school on an obviously broken leg, his head at a grotesque 90-degree angle, like he's taking a nap on his own shoulder. We keep talking about going out to kill him, but there haven't been many volunteers for that job.

To say food is running low is an understatement. We scrounged and stockpiled food from everyone's lunches and long ago went on room-to-room scouting missions to grab snacks stashed in teachers' drawers. Don't even ask what else we found buried in some of those drawers. Still, with tight-fisted rationing, we don't have much left. Once the food runs out, the options left for us aren't really options at all: Either we venture into the teachers' lounge, where we know there's food, or try to escape through the horde. I think we've all learned through the acts of our parents, though, that that's plain stupid.

No one knows what to do.

We hoped our parents would come. We hoped someone – anyone – would save us. What else can we hope for?

I've been described as mature for my age and I get good grades. I'm one of the oldest kids here, but I'm only 14.

I don't know what to do. Please come help us. Please.

LOCAL HERO

by
Rajiv Moté

The shield rested atop a pedestal behind a cordon of Elvish rope. Angled for display, it was dented, blackened and completely melted around the edges. It was beautiful. Garga yearned to touch it. But the Elf guard standing to the side had a long, curved blade at his belt – the enchanted, Orc-killing kind. Garga kept his hands at his sides.

Orcs milled about the gallery's length, between the shield and the great statue of Borag at the other end. This part of the museum was free to enter, and the Men, Elves and Dwarves visiting or settling the Black Land favored the other galleries that displayed the trophies of their own people from the war against the Dark Lord. This place was for Orcs. No longer was there an army, nor lash, nor much of anything for Orc-folk to do. Without the army, the clans were assigned no lands, and forbidden weapons, there was no way to lay claim to any. So Orcs simply wandered the Black Land, and the museum was as good a place to escape the sun as any cave. Here, they could meet and grouse during the worst of the heat, and even under the eyes of the conquerors, they felt this place theirs. Where else were there Orc-things to be found on pedestals in this occupied land?

Across the gallery from Garga stood Sheketh's massive statue of Borag the Liberator, down on one knee, muscles coiled with power, his massive arms holding up his great shield to the sky as if to blot out the sun. Borag the Rebel, who defied the Dark Lord and shepherded the Halflings to the very Mountain of Fire, destroying the tyrant's power and freeing the Black Land. Borag the Defiant, who lifted the Halflings on his shield to their rescue, even as a molten river consumed him, leaving only his shield to tell the story.

The statue was proud and powerful, but Garga liked Borag's shield better. It was real. Every time he saw it – and he came to see it often – it reminded him of something so easy to forget. Orcs fought the Dark Lord too. Orcs, who suffered under him more than any other people, fought back. Orcs had heroes. Garga knew that the real Borag probably looked nothing like the statue. Some gaffers even said it revealed Sheketh's shame of being an Orc. Its back was straight, like a Man's, and its features too fine, almost beautiful, like an Elf's. The real Borag was a soldier. He would have had scars and broken bones, ill-healed, like all the old gaffers who survived the war. Garga had never seen an Orc like the one across the hall, carved larger than life in black basalt. But the shield… That shield had seen battle. It had stopped axes and swords. It had survived the fires of the mountain. Not beautiful, but resilient. It was a thing of Orc-folk, given a place of honor where nothing Orcish was honored.

If only Garga could touch it.

He could lean across the rope, reach with his fingertips, and then run. He could duck underneath, then back, fast and silent as wind. But every time he visited, he lost his nerve. Even here, especially here, Orcs knew to walk small. It made the blood pound in his neck and stirred his limbs with restless energy. His forehead felt hot. A young Orc he knew once said, "Fish don't know water, just as Orcs don't know shame."

"You do realize it's all nonsense," rang a clear, sing-song voice from across the room. Two Elf youths were standing in front of the statue. The Orcs gave them a wide berth. "Borag probably didn't even exist." The youth who spoke – boy, girl, Garga couldn't tell Elves apart – acted as though they were talking to their friend, but that ringing voice could be heard throughout the hall. The friend laughed, an irritating, bird-pitched titter.

The Orcs averted their eyes. A few grumbled, but not loudly.

"A beaten people must try to salvage their pride. A broken sword. A half-melted shield. Entire mythologies are woven from such detritus."

Now there was no grumbling. There was

scarcely the sound of breath. Garga glanced at the guard. The corners of his mouth seemed to want to twitch upward. Garga's parents had drilled the lesson into him: this was bait for a trap. The Orc that took it would be beaten bloody, if not killed outright.

A grizzled old Orc near Garga said, "Shut your filthy gob." He was a warrior, probably even a veteran of the War.

The Orcs around him moved back, leaving him alone. Exposed. Garga, shame and fear pounding in his ears, backed up against the rope.

The Elf youths glided across the room, parting the crowd. "What did you say, old goat?"

There was nothing Garga nor anyone else could do. His people were forbidden weapons, and those charged with their protection were just as likely to strike blows of their own. The old Orc was finished.

Every Orc in the Black Land learned a sort of fatalism about Elves, Men, and Dwarves after the war. But around the edges of that fatalism was an unnamable feeling, at once wild, dangerous and exciting. A drawn bowstring feeling of waiting.

Leaning back against the rope, Garga reached backward, straining for contact with that blackened, holy piece of metal. A clever Orc seized opportunities.

"Shut. Your. Filthy. Gob."

He was a brave one, this old-timer. And most likely a dead one. The veterans usually wanted to die.

Garga looked at the guard out of the corner of his eye. He was watching the confrontation with mild interest. His long, delicate fingers brushed his sword hilt.

The Elf youths circled the old-timer like buzzards circling a kill, buzzards that looked like swans, standing taller than their intended prey. But these Elves were no warriors.

It happened all at once. A leg hooked behind a knee sent one Elf onto his back. A fist gnarled as old roots drove up under the chin of the other. The crowd surged backward. Garga tumbled over the rope. A sword left its sheath with a ring like a whistling kettle. The silence broke with the roars of dozens of Orcs. The old warrior knelt astride a prone Elf, beating his face bloody while the other youth tried to pull him off. He'd have a better chance moving a boulder. The guard glided toward them, the naked blade in his hand shining with cold, painful light. He raised it almost lazily into the air.

It fell with a dull thunk against dented, blackened metal. Garga felt the force of the blow from wrist to shoulder, but the shield held. Again and again the blade fell, darting from new angles. Garga desperately moved, keeping the blade from touching the old-timer. He heard a roar, a warrior's roar, and realized with a thrill that it came from his own throat. The Elf drew back his arm again, and Garga showed his teeth, steeling himself for the next blow.

Maybe Orcs had no true history to warrant pride. Maybe Borag never existed. But his shield was real. So was the courage it inspired. And every Orc who escaped this gallery would tell the story of how Garga used it.

WEEDS AND SEEDS

by
Mariah Montoya

The girl and her new boyfriend, Caden, were sending kissing emojis back and forth when she noticed the first weed poking through her pillow's lacy case like a naughty feather.

It was a thistle, and as the girl watched, round-eyed, the thistle wiggled upward, its spikes like tentacles reaching out to grab her.

The girl dropped her phone on her pink bedspread, picked it up again, and texted Caden, "gtg. found a weed in my room. blah!"

Before she raced downstairs to find Mom's gardening gloves, her phone lit up again with Caden's reply: "ok, I'll be waiting for you, baby" with a zany face next to it and a purple heart.

The girl bolted downstairs, where she rummaged through laundry room drawers. From the kitchen, Mom called, "Dinner's almost ready, Holly! Get your brother for me, won't you?"

"Can't, Mom," the girl said breathlessly.

Her fingers dug through the junk drawer, throwing aside dud flashlights and useless bits of string and dead batteries. *Why* Dad kept all this junk, she'd never know…

Then she found the rubber gloves, snatched them and raced back upstairs, ignoring Mom's protests. A roast was sizzling in the slow cooker, but she ignored its tangy smells too. She burst into her bedroom, ready to pull the damned thistle by its spiky roots.

The girl dropped her gloves.

In her two-minute absence, more weeds had cropped up.

They peeped from the cracks in her dresser, from the spine of her abandoned Geometry book, from the pile of clothes on her moon chair that she had meant to fold. Dandelions had ripped from the carpet. Crabgrass had sprouted from the windowsill and now curtained the windowpane. What looked horribly like poison ivy had burst from within her cell phone itself, cracking the screen and twining its roots around her glittered phone case.

"Shit!" the girl screamed, deciding that this was a good time to cuss. She couldn't get in trouble for cussing when weeds throttled her bedroom. "Shit!" she screamed again.

Footsteps thumped up the stairs, across the hall and to her bedroom.

Mom stood in the doorway, her mouth hanging open. She folded her arms and pursed her lips. "Holly, what's this rubbish? I thought I told you to keep it pure in here?"

"I… I didn't do it," the girl said. Really? How unfair. Why would she have planted weeds in every crevice of her personal life, on every surface of her personal space?

"I won't tolerate this, Holly." Mom tapped her sandal against a thick mass of clovers. "Find a way to get rid of it, okay? By this weekend. Now come on and eat dinner."

The girl stammered, but after a quick meal of roast beef and sautéed green beans, she used the family phone to call Lawn Maintenance, who said that a bedroom didn't count as a lawn. Then she called Pest Control, who said that thistles didn't count as pests. Finally, she called Mold Removal, who told her that she must not know the difference between mold, mildew and milkweed, but that they were *so* glad to be of service, and Have A Good Day.

The girl sat on her bed, stumped, kicking away vines that snaked around her wrists and tried chaining her to the headboard.

She could hear her brother shouting at his video game controller from down the hall and Mom talking to Dad on the phone downstairs: "… just don't know what's gotten into her lately. Weeds everywhere, Jeremy! They're hanging from her light fixture! Yes, I'd stop by a hardware store on your way back. Buy some new light bulbs."

While it was a comfort to know that Dad would buy her some light bulbs, the girl cried into her fingers. Her stomach roiled as if a clump of ferns might be brewing in there. Her nose felt plugged by chickweed. Her heart felt cracked by burdock. Mid-cry, however, she realized her tears were watering the pillow thistle, which had grown so tall it brushed the ceiling plaster.

Angry now, the girl ripped vines off her ankles and tore downstairs and outside, where she marched to Dad's shed.

It was dark out now. She hadn't finished her homework, because the weeds had swallowed it. Caden would be wondering where she was, because the weeds had swallowed her phone. She hadn't picked an outfit for tomorrow, because the weeds had swallowed her laundry. She needed to extinguish the beasts, now, before they swallowed *her*.

The girl found a half-empty container of herbicide jammed in the shed corner behind Dad's lawnmower. She trooped back to her bedroom with a raised chin, avoiding Mom's sharp gaze. She was about to unleash the entire poisonous contents upon her room when she realized that the herbicide might end up killing her too.

Exhausted, weighed down by the grave state of her bedroom, which looked like a tangled, thorny monster's belly, the girl slunk downstairs for the last time and approached Mom, who was loading the dishwasher with soapy hands.

"Can you help me, Mom?"

"What do you need, Holly?"

"I need flower seeds. Do you have any left over from when you planted your garden?"

Mom led her to the laundry room again,

where, under the mud sink, she retrieved a box stuffed with seed packets – magnolias, dahlias, daylilies, hollyhocks, marigolds. Holly hugged the packets to her chest and returned to her room. She sprinkled the seeds over her carpet and dresser and bed. Then she stuffed a handful of seeds into her lacy pillowcase for good measure.

As the flowers budded and bloomed across her room, pale pink and violet and gold, the girl donned her dropped rubber gloves, ready to rip out the weeds by their roots, one at a time.

CASTRATI

by
Bryan Miller

My mother dreamed I had the perfect voice.

That hope kept her eyes forward and held her chin still while she watched the doctor's assistant hold my skinny limbs straight when I began to buck and jolt. The surgeon's knife would trap the high tone of that scream I screamed, stop it in time forever.

Between my legs, I felt the scalpel's edge bite through skin and loops of sinew. The pain boiled up through my stomach and flooded my head. The doctor jerked his wet hand away in a hot gush. I spit out the gnawed wooden stick between my teeth and heaved up all the brandy they'd given me for anesthetic. As I fainted, I saw my mother nod.

She was right.

I had joined the ranks of the castrato, those heavenly singers whose bloody sacrifice halted the putrid pubescence that alters their perfect young voices. Now my throat's organ was the center of me. The clear, high sounds it piped out flitted across every trill and roulade to a crystalline pitch that could freeze a room's oxygen.

It no longer mattered that I was lowborn, from a town too far outside the city to call myself a Florentine. In the opera houses across Europe, I could summon Rossini's Count Almaviva and Mozart's Countess Almaviva as equally as if one were my left hand and the other my right. My voice milked tears from men's eyes, unlatched their pocketbooks, reverberated through the hollows of doorlocks until they clicked open. For me.

Then one night, in preparation for the opening of *Fidelio* at the Palais Garnier, I felt a spasm of agony in that soft hollow between my thighs, a pain that reminded me of the last day I was just another farmer's son.

I staggered to my dressing room to tug off my costume and there found something impossible: a full new scrotum, pink and hairless as a piglet's belly, bulging through the white crook of scar tissue below my manhood. The ovoid growths inside were swollen and pupal. Through the translucent balloon of skin, I could make out their intricate ridges of aching vein.

And I could feel them elsewhere, too. Higher up, in my throat. Their fine tendrils yanking down on my delicate instrument. I was certain I could feel Orfeo's lament dying in my mouth.

In a panic, right there in the dressing room, I did my best to replicate the doctor's procedure of so long ago. While a tea spoon heated over an uncovered lamp's flame, I used a loose snippet of harpsichord wire to tie off this raw bulge between my legs. I cinched the wire noose tighter, tighter, until the agonizing pinch flattened to thrumming numbness.

I fumbled a straight razor from my toiletry kit.

I had no assistant to hold me down, only speed and determination. I leaned forward to rest the damned full scrotum atop the white-painted oak top of my dressing table. I took a deep breath and closed my eyes. Then I drew the straight razor sideways hard enough to leave a deep gouge in the wood below.

For a moment, I went blind with the awfulness of it.

Somehow, my limbs carried out the rest of the procedure. I burned three fingers on my right hand as I reached for the blazing spoon. Then I pressed its sizzling convex backside deep into my fresh rupture. All this, just as I passed out. Elsewise, I would have bled to death.

Perhaps I should have died of the infection, too, but I did not. I returned to the stage a week later, following two performances from my understudy. The applause was so loud when I stepped into the Garnier's footlights, the understudy quit on the spot.

I could never abandon that feeling, even after so many more years of gorging on it. Just as certainly as I could never force myself to perform that hideous surgery on myself again.

I tell you all this by way of explanation.

Yes, sir, I will perform for you an Emone that

not even Traetta himself could have dreamed when he conjured the notes. I will sing for your crowds.

But first, I have a problem to be solved. You must accompany me to my dressing room, and take this razor, and be my hands.

MOONLIT PROPOSAL

by
Jen Sexton-Riley

Part of me feels embarrassed. It's so old-fashioned. So old-school traditional. This could go either way. Trina may be bowled over by the romance or… I don't know, dropped flat by the olden-days mustiness of it all.

Only one way to find out.

The velvet cube in my pocket makes my pants fit funny. A misplaced bulge.

"Hey, Alix! Happy to see me, girl?" I can imagine Trina saying, lowering her chin and raising her eyebrows, eyeing my lopsided package.

I smile. My cheeks burn slightly. Who'd have dreamed I'd one day be loved so intimately, know someone's mind so thoroughly that even when I'm all alone, I blush at what she'd be likely to say?

The cube is not a happy bulge, but a hinged box of deepest red, which cracks itself across and opens all the way in half, as my heart has thrown itself wide for Trina. The glinting, precious thing inside is for her alone, the choice hers alone to make.

Oh, my early intentions were all about caution and sensibility. But now? Sensibility went for a long walk when Trina strode smiling into my life.

And here she comes through the trees, trotting in the darkness up the hill's curving path in her knee-high black boots. Her braids bounce, half caught up in a knot on the back of her head.

"There you are, Mx. Mysterioso!" She throws her arms around me. Kisses me. Nips my throat. She doesn't know that every movement is becoming a memory I'll call upon for reassurance in the years to come. "What the hell are we doing up here in the dark, anyway? It'll start raining any minute," she says, grinning and shaking her head at me. "I didn't even know the park gates were open this late."

I can't help but laugh. I close my eyes and take a deep breath. "Trina, there's something I want to ask you here. Where we met," I say, my voice measured and low.

I take her hand and sink to one knee. She gasps, hops backward, stammers some jumbled obscenities. Her voice squeaks. The night shines in her wide eyes, glints on the sharpness of her smile.

"Trina, I can't imagine facing the end of my life without you. Since the moment we met I knew. You have the passion, the courage to be there for me in a way nobody else could ever be. I love you, Trina. I trust you. I know what I'm about to ask you isn't easy, but I can't imagine asking anyone else. Trina…"

The wind shifts the clouds, releasing a sliver of moonlight. It spills across Trina's face and drags a delicious claw of desire through my heart.

My breath sinks to a rumble deep in my throat. "Trina, someday far in the future, when you know the time is right…"

I open the box. Nestled in the black velvet lies a single silver bullet.

"Trina," I snarl. "Will you?"

TIME AND TIDE

by
Chrissie Rohrman

The shaman's fingertips trailed the puckered ridge that ran the length of Talia's left arm, scrutinizing the cursed wound. As she awaited his diagnosis, she felt the ever-present tug of dark magic spreading slowly through her veins and threatening her life.

She'd nearly reached the shores of Anchora when Athan's people found her. She had known the risk of fleeing, of breaking the magical oath that bound her to the ruthless warlock.

The attack spell should have killed her instantly. Instead, death was her constant companion, lingering just out of eyeshot. Perhaps death was what she was owed, for all the pain and suffering she'd caused as one of Athan's mercenaries.

Talia's hand rested on her swollen belly. She wasn't that woman anymore, wanted a better life now. She *needed* it, for Leah, the daughter she carried, the unexpected condition that had caused her to run.

She'd traveled for weeks, by cover of night, to reach this rumored place of healing. Her hope of a second chance lay with the shaman.

She inhaled sharply as the old man pressed a tender spot. She gazed down at her mangled arm and wondered if he could tell who she'd been. She wondered if it would affect his decision, if he could sense whether she was worth more in life or death.

The shaman released Talia's arm and lowered his hunched body to a well-worn cushion. "It cannot be undone. This magic has dug in too deeply."

Dread settled in Talia's chest. She bit her lip and tugged at the hem of her long, loose sleeve, covering the scars. "How long?"

Moonlight streamed through the thatched roof, exaggerating the deep wrinkles on either side of his wide mouth. "Five years."

No. Was that her curse, to leave her daughter motherless?

Talia dropped to her knees. "There must be something–"

He lifted a hand. "It cannot be undone. But it can be transferred."

Talia swallowed. He was proposing a deal. A trade. Her life for that of another. An echo of the life she'd left behind. "How?"

The shaman pressed a weighty gold coin into her palm. It burned with an intense heat that seemed to be pulled from the magic writhing within her arm. "You have until the coin loses its value entirely to pass the curse to another."

She shook her head. "I don't understand."

"You came here to save yourself." His voice was a soft scrape of sound, and his wizened features held no expression. "I have given you that chance. But if you are still holding the coin when its value is gone, then this curse is yours alone to bear."

Talia closed her fingers around the coin and nodded.

The old man lifted a gnarled hand and blew across his palm, exhaling a plume of dust into her face.

She turned away with a wince, sneezing as the peppery powder invaded her senses. When she worked her eyes open, she was no longer crouched in the hut, but in the middle of a sunny, bustling marketplace.

Light-headed and disoriented, Talia rose. Bodies pressed against her from all sides as people rushed about the crowded, hazy bazaar. Their voices mashed into a dull murmur, everyone speaking in languages she couldn't name.

In a sort of dream state, she looked down at the coin in her hand, dismayed to see the golden piece had turned into a shining bit of silver. She was already running out of time.

Just pick someone.

Talia propelled herself forward, wading into the throng of marketplace patrons. She didn't recognize anyone in the oppressive crowd, could hardly even discern features. A giggling child dashed past and she backed away, her fingers tightening around the enchanted coin. There had

to be a thief among them. A murderer.
There is.
No.
She'd done awful things while in Athan's employ, but she'd never killed directly. It had been bad enough, and Talia was terrified of that life being all she was. If she passed off this curse, she'd be forced to live with the knowledge she'd damned another poor soul to die within five years.

But she'd *live*. She'd have a new, better life with her daughter.

Pick someone.

She clenched her jaw, steeled her resolve.

A figure in a long, hooded cloak brushed Talia's cursed arm. She closed her eyes and gripped the person's hand, forced the coin between their fingers.

It's done.

Talia opened her eyes, but as the figure – her victim – dropped their hood, it wasn't relief that washed over her.

She found herself facing a young woman with olive skin and piercing green eyes and a dull copper coin in her hand. No more than nineteen and familiar in a way that tore at Talia's heart. She'd never seen the woman before, yet she *knew* her. They locked eyes, the moment lasting too long and not long enough.

"Leah?" Talia whispered, knowing the answer already. The name she'd picked for her unborn daughter. Her mother's name, in hopes some of the woman's good, pure nature would pass on instead of her own wickedness.

She stumbled back, knowing she'd made an awful mistake.

Around her, faces were coming into focus. She spotted her father, her childhood friend Laris over the young woman's shoulder. The large, hulking form of Athan. People from her past, her present, her future. Not a stranger among them, and all staring with accusation in their eyes. She should have known the shaman's magic, his help, would come with a catch.

Talia shook her head in denial and pawed at the young woman, desperate to recover the coin, the curse, the pain.

A sudden tug backward tore Leah from her grasp, and Talia from the shaman's vision.

The dim room spun around her as she came back to herself, to reality.

Talia pushed up on trembling arms, hot tears on her cheeks. The magical coin was gone, her palm empty. She drew up her sleeve, revealing smooth skin. "What did you do?" she shouted.

"I offered you a chance," the shaman replied calmly.

"Send me back there," she pleaded, wrapping her unmarred arm protectively around the bulge at her middle. "I'll give it to someone else."

The old man's face was solemn. "It is done."

"No," she whispered hoarsely.

All she'd wanted was more time with Leah. A sharp pain bit from deep inside as the curse took hold of her precious daughter, her chance at a do-over, who would not live to see her fifth year, because of her.

Talia knew now where her worth was.

THE OVEN IN THE WOODS

by
Alexander Langer

The old woman took a drag on her cigarette. It tasted horrible, the vegetal stink of tobacco supplemented by ersatz wartime ingredients. It gave her something to do with her hands, though, and blunted her sense of smell.

She coughed. This deep in the forest, they didn't need to worry about being overheard. No one came here, not even the Schutzstaffel.

Behind her, the cottage door opened with a creaking whine, and she tensed momentarily, before she felt a familiar hand rest gently on her shoulder. Her muscles relaxed, and she closed her eyes. "Tea, Grete?" asked her husband.

She turned into Albert's arms. His cheeks might be hollow from hunger and his hairline disintegrating like a sandbar in a North Sea gale, but in her mind, he was as handsome as the day she'd met him. His gold-rimmed eyeglasses accentuated his warm brown eyes, still sparkling with humor despite everything. She traced the crooked and beloved arch of his nose with her finger. Years of snoring, but she wouldn't change a thing.

"Yes, *danke schoen*," Grete said, smiling.

She joined him inside, where the small wood stove was heating the water for their forest-harvested chamomile. The old thing was worth all the trouble of hauling it through the woods to this godforsaken place, despite how slow it had made them. She wouldn't touch the cottage's ancient bread oven. Even being in its presence...

She shuddered. It has been sixty years, but the smell, like pork left to roast for too long, permeated everything.

When the tea was ready, they returned to the decaying front porch and the cool night breeze. After a long moment, he said, "I'm sorry, Grete. For all of this."

She sighed. This was a well-worn argument. "Nonsense," she replied.

Albert responded by wrapping his arm around her. She leaned into him and closed her eyes to hold back the tears. Had it been easy for him, loving the girl who'd come back from the witch's forest, the smell of smoke lingering in her hair? She knew her own jagged edges well enough to know it hadn't. Had treasured his love even more because of it.

When he'd been taken by grim men in black uniforms, she'd never thought to see him again. But he'd come back, returned from the dead on her doorstep in the night, ragged and hollow-eyed. She would be his rock now. If it meant returning here, where no one came, to protect him, so be it.

No matter how many times he made the trip, the trees always felt too close. Their branches and leaves wove together in a hushed conspiracy to erase the sky.

The old man dropped another smooth white pebble, to mark his way back if the path vanished or changed. Maybe all forests resisted being known, but this one refused to be mapped even more than most.

It had been six decades since he'd first wandered here. He thought the trees would be used to his presence by now, an old acquaintance if not a friend. But each time he could feel their disquiet and scheming malevolence. He returned not because he wanted to, but because his sister, his heart, was here.

Their father had been a tyrant and a weak man, in thrall to his appetites, far more concerned with whether his wage from the lumberyard could buy another bottle of schnapps or a night at the bordello than food for his motherless children. So, when the pretty young woman with the tawny eyes whispered in his ear that his twin son and daughter would make fine assistants for her work, he eagerly agreed. He'd taken them deep into the wood and left them with her, despite her carnivorous smile and cabin that smelled of sweet ginger and something foul.

There, the horror that defined their lives had

happened. What only he and his sister understood.

Screaming and the smell of burning flesh flitted across the old man's mind. He shuddered. He was almost there.

#

Grete heard her brother winding through the trees well before she saw him. Few animals came near the ruined cabin: when the tawny-eyed witch had lacked her favorite prey, she'd hunted for the furred young under the trees, and the forest remembered.

Hans looked haggard just like her. They had the same blue eyes and once-sandy-now-grey hair, the same pinched jaw and pensive brow. He carried an overstuffed rucksack, which he placed in front of them and opened up. There were potatoes and onions and root vegetables, and bones for a stock. They had tried to plant their own food, but nothing edible grew in the witch's garden. Only wrinkled fruit that rotted on the vine and smelled of sulfur.

"More rationing," he said, by way of explanation. "And they took the fifteen-year-olds for the *Volkssturm*."

Grete's stomach churned, with loathing and fear and despair. With nothing else to say, she asked, "Will you stay for supper?"

#

Hans sipped his soup. His brother-in-law sat next to him as they huddled around the stove. Albert pulled up the sleeves of his jacket and shivered. Through his arm hair, Hans saw the blue-ink numbers on his forearm.

Hans had never married. The only way to ensure he would not be like his father – his weak, vicious father – was if he never became one at all. Grete had taken another road and married a man who was nothing like their father. Soft-handed where their father was callused. Educated when he was a simpleton. Gentle and temperate when he was an angry drunk.

A Jew, when their father had hated them.

Albert was a good man, proud of his service to the Kaiser and Fatherland. He stayed when things started to get bad. It would pass, he said. Grete had broken when he was taken, her eyes as haunted as when they'd escaped the wood as children. It was a miracle when Albert had returned, emaciated and dreaming of burning flesh, but alive. His fatherland had sold him to the black-clad witches, with their Totenkopfs and guns. He knew now what Hans and Grete knew. Fathers and fatherlands could not be relied upon for safety in this world.

They'd fled to the woods and the house with its rotting candy lintels and half-decayed sugar windows, hiding in a dead nightmare to avoid a living one.

As the sun began its descent and the sky glowed gold, the shadow of the oven fell over the trio. The forbidding brick structure filled the center of the cottage, its cast-iron door rusting away on its hinges, the witch's pounding and screaming against its walls ringing in Hans' ears. Hans kept his eyes off of it and saw that Grete and Albert did the same.

Instead, they stared into the setting sun.

No one said anything. There was nothing to say.

FORGIVE THE ADORING BEAST

by
Hailey Piper

Love kept me going even when my witch killed me, and she killed me many times.

I didn't know the shores were hers that first time. I had finished eating a creature of fire and bones and descended to the white beach to wash its blood off my hands. A morose whistle drew me along the shoreline while my fingers still dripped red.

I wouldn't have chosen to show myself that way to her, but I thought the whistle meant food. I followed it to a narrow crack between slanted stones and slipped inside, skin greased with serpent gristle.

Hides of long-dead animals draped her shoulders, mementos of the old world. A small fire lit her cavern and breathed violet smoke. Its light reflected off glass jars where brown buds festered, efforts to grow things in dead soil.

Pitiful, I thought. To tear and eat her insides would be a mercy.

She growled and charged at me. "My home. Mine!"

I stumbled back, stunned. Things didn't run at me; they ran from me. I wasn't prepared.

Her fingers latched around my head and dragged me outside, where she broke every bone in my body and threw me to the waves.

Recovery took days. I spent them thinking of she who had bested me – *me*, devourer of species! Worse, she had bewitched my long-rotted heart. Her hides enchanted greater than my animal nakedness, and her silver eyes – inescapable.

I crawled on hands and knees back to the mouth of her cavern and begged acceptance. She sighed, bared her teeth and murdered me.

Days later, I washed ashore and tried again. I welcomed every death, but to earn her tenderness, I'd have starved.

And I never starve.

But I could share. I found a man and woman in the southern wastelands, where they dug beneath petrified trees for subterranean fruit. Gifts.

Once they were dead, I carried them to her home. Violet smoke swept from its mouth, and my witch stared despondent at the sea. What good timing. Look at my bloody hands; what I've done to please you!

She flashed tearful eyes, then wrathful, and again broke my bones and discarded me. Black water bloated my body. I was sick for many seasons before I returned. I wished she'd eaten my gifts, but that wasn't her nature.

I tried simpler gifts then. Insects, shellfish – anything that might please her better. If she'd torn me open and feasted on my bones, it would have been a pleasure. The end of me – to be digested means no return – but we'd be one forever.

Always the same. Bones broken, cast into the sea.

Before long, she wasn't angry anymore. She was busy with her impossible task, and I'd become a nuisance, typical as tide and storms. Why couldn't she understand? We two were alike in this dead world.

But I realized it was I who'd misunderstood. She was as special as me and needed a gift just as grand.

A god, perhaps? Yes, my teeth had experience with gods.

I found one sleeping atop a glistening glass plateau. Kneeling skeletons encircled it, its followers who'd starved to death in worship. It reminded me of younger days, everyone else praying and fasting while I uncovered the graves of dead gods and gnawed at their god-rotted entrails.

None joined me then, but perhaps my witch could. Had she, too, eaten of gods? We could share this one together.

I tore off its head.

Kneeling outside her home, I begged her attention. The horned head pulsed between my fingers, silver blood streaming down my forearms.

She emerged with an exhausted grimace. I'd

come at a poor time and looked down, ready to be broken and cast away.

Instead, weight lifted from my hands. Her hand passed over each side of the head, forcing its eyes shut, and then she snarled at me. A love snarl? "You'll do harm until I make use of you, it seems. Follow."

I stood, shaking, and padded after her. At last, my witch wanted me.

We climbed the slanted stones, where at the top stood an ivory tree that snatched the sun in its branches. She laid me between its roots.

"Rest now, little famine," she whispered.

Tender fingers coaxed me into loving sleep. We were one in that moment, and because time cannot be changed, it was forever, too.

I slept through her cracking the horn off the god's head, loud as thunder, and slashing open my side. Her nails gutted me, leaving a meaty hide. She slathered the dead god's silver blood across my skin and hung me from the tree to dry. Then she left.

She must've buried the head below; I smelled god-rot in autumn. In winter, it promised new life in the world, that though I was a wretched, ravenous beast, I had done one thing right. I swore if I ever healed, I would devour that head.

But its promise came true in a way I didn't expect – my witch returned.

When spring came, she climbed the tree, whistling the same keen tune I'd heard when we first met. Gentle hands took my now-brittle skin, crackling at every touch, and crushed it into powder. Hearty winds tore my pieces through tree branches, and at last, I understood what she'd done. Witch, god, sun and tree had transformed me into life-giving spores.

We were bringing back the world.

I despaired. My dust would bring all manner of flora and fauna, all horribly alive. Their genesis would digest me, and I would cease to be.

But then my pieces smiled together in their last memory of teeth. My witch had toiled at remaking the world. At last, her work would bear fruit. Our work. I'd helped bring her joy.

Better still, no wastelands meant no peace. When all things returned to life, such violence they would visit on each other, endless eons of bloodshed. My witch and I made this together.

If that isn't love, I don't know what is.

COYOTE-FACED WOMAN

by
Marissa James

This is how the coyote-faced woman became coyote-faced:

A man from the city across the waters caught her gathering reeds on the shore. He flayed the skin from her body, from the top of her head to her feet. All night beneath the witnessing moon, he danced in her skin and howled sorcery to the sky. The woman lay helpless and wept tears that seared her fleshless face.

When morning came and he had no more use for it, the man returned her skin, but by then it was in tatters.

The man killed a passing coyote and, wherever he had danced away her skin he put patches of coyote hide. He gave her the paws in place of hands. Her face was entirely gone, so he gave her the face of the coyote. Then he went back across the waters and left her there.

#

This is what happened to the coyote-faced woman after she became coyote-faced:

She returned home. Villagers fled, but her mother and brothers knew her by a birthmark on her tattered human skin. When she tried to tell what had happened only the growls and slaver of a beast came forth. When she tried to draw in the dirt her coyote paws were clumsy and useless. Her coyote eyes could not weep, so she whimpered her despair.

Her brothers declared their right to blood-payment as though she was dead, but who would truly challenge a sorcerer from that strange, wicked place across the waters? Her coyote nose smelled her mother's sorrow and the mingled disgust and pity of the villagers she had known all her life.

Perhaps it was the way she pawed at closed doors like a dog, or the way her ears pricked at distant noises, that drew fear like an eclipse over her village. Or perhaps her slavering coyote face reminded them of what lay so close beyond the water.

Her body changed in other ways, too, and though she had never been with child, she knew the signs. Before this, too, could become a source of pity and loathing, she returned to the shore, to the place of the bones of the flayed coyote.

With that cold company in the swaying reeds she called for the man from across the waters.

How to beg him to undo his sorcery when she could not speak? Would he find pity and change her back or, in disgust, make an end to the suffering he created? The moon hung low over her back and she howled to the sky in despair. Beyond the murmuring of the reeds, a coyote replied; or perhaps it was her own echo.

She awoke with the morning to see a large canoe approaching. A man strode through the rowers and disembarked.

She knew the man by his body that once fit inside her skin. Her coyote nose knew his scent; her blood and that of the dead coyote, faint and mixed with sorcery. Her belly roiled at the sight of him, but the coyote nature in her calmed this wrath with a low, warning growl. She must wait.

He stood before her in a splendor of quetzal feathers and jaguar skin, not the blood and mud she remembered. The copper and jade of his jewelry shone in the morning like stars around the bleak center of the galaxy.

"I know you, coyote-faced woman," he said. "You are the one in whose skin I danced beneath the witnessing moon. Now see what I have become because of it. I am the lord of the people who dwell across the water. I have come to take you with me, coyote-faced woman, for you are a symbol of my power."

She could not say yes and she could not say no, so she stepped into the canoe with him and they went across the waters.

#

This is how the coyote-faced woman birthed her revenge:

The people did not live across the water but in the middle of it. In every direction, water stretched around their heaping mud city, except where a bridge met the nearest marshy land.

From her cell, she witnessed the strange ways of these people. They ate the flesh of rats and captives, and weeds dredged from the murky water. They built houses of skulls and longbones, animal and human, and fed offal to the gardens so that even ripe squashes stank of carcass. The lord did not allow her among the people but kept her confined, like a tethered dog, to display the fearful possibilities of his sorcery to courtiers and commanders.

Because the lord otherwise neglected her existence, the coyote-faced woman did little but contemplate the stone walls her world and future had become. She counted the cycles of the moon and stroked her belly with coyote paws as the two waxed to fullness together. She whimpered to think of her family, her people, but tempered the desire to return with the memory of her mother's sorrow, her brothers' rage and despair.

After eight months, she collapsed with pain. She whimpered and clawed the floor, her body writhing under skin that was half hers and half coyote. She would be flayed again, this time from the inside, and she willed it to happen if only it would make an end to her misery.

As though it understood her wish, the coyote

nature inside her bore its teeth and rose. Labor pangs became flint shards knifing her gut. She raised her muzzle and howled to the witnessing moon.

The coyote-faced woman birthed a surging, tooth-glinting pack of coyote. Conceived by the sorcery that had shorn away her humanity, nurtured on sorrow and rage, they were hungry and vengeful and swift.

From outside came a familiar sound; the howl of a coyote, then another and another. Down the bridge all the coyote of the world ran, a torrent of feral shape and moon-bright teeth that had come to her call. They flooded the streets and tore apart the people.

The pack born of her body used their coyote paws to bear down the door and their coyote noses to scent out the lord and his kin and their coyote teeth to flay them alive. Not a one escaped, for the eight months she had carried them made her coyote children more powerful than any sorcery danced under a single phase of the moon.

The coyote-faced woman watched it all. She saw the beauty and grace of the coyote, her pack-children the most beautiful among them – but surely, her motherly eye was partial.

When the screams and howls faded into stillness, she joined her pack. A sheen of blood illuminated the city. Tatters of bone and flesh littered the streets. From alleys and windows and rooftops, coyote eyes shone, ten thousand tiny moons glinting with welcome, for, to coyote eyes, she was not fearful to behold. To coyote ears, her growls and whimpers were speech, responded to in kind. Deep within, her coyote nature gave a contented sigh.

Among her kin, the coyote-faced woman danced through blood beneath the gaze of the witnessing moon.

THE PORTRAIT IN THE PINES

by
Kurt Newton

I. Lucy Jane

With summer long lost, the icy flows of autumn invaded the deep pinewoods.

Caleb John, free from want but wretched in need, alone in his artist's retreat, fed the fire to try and rid the shack of painful memories.

A portrait sat above the mantle, staring lovely. A whisper smile, raven hair and skin so soft and white. Lucy Jane, his heart's companion, lost like summer long, the pines the last to see her.

Every day, in rain or shine, Caleb walked the wooded needle-path in hopes of finding something telling: a strand of hair, a strip of cloth, the pale exposure of a slender hand. But nothing ever showed.

Some days, he'd stop inside the clearing – for carrying such a heavy heart is tiring – and alone he'd sit among the pines that filtered green the cold light through, and dream of warmer days when laughter danced upon the boughs and every moment was an eternity lost to love.

Memories of his Lucy Jane, so natural and pure, the perfect lover, the perfect wife. Never had the end to his loneliness seemed so permanent. Until that summer day when he wanted nothing more than to capture his Lucy Jane in oils, painting pretty that which captured him.

But Lucy Jane, as shy as she was beautiful, was adamant he never try, warning him with tender lips that she was meant for his eyes only. But Caleb, an artist born, could not resist and therefore hatched a clever plan.

A picnic in the clearing. And afterwards, as he stood painting summer pines and Lucy Jane lay fast asleep upon the needle bed, he would quietly turn his easel from one beauty to another.

All was fine, until halfway through, the daylight seemed to pull away, the pines grew dark, and Lucy Jane, suddenly awakened, her whisper smile sad but still, rooted to her portrait place, began to fade.

But Caleb, lost in his artist's spell, failed to see his love's reflection leave and only thought it rude of her to abandon him so close to the portrait's end.

Angrily, he packed his easel, thinking silly her escape, and walked the home path, sure to find her waiting. But the shack was an empty host, its pinewood walls and pinewood floors eerily a-shiver, as if a woman's touch had never been... and would never be again.

All that night, Caleb, lost in a frenzied craze, crissed and crossed the pinewood paths by moonlight, calling for his heart's companion, only to hear the moaning of the pines and the echo of his lone and sorrowful voice.

And even now, with summer lost to autumn, Caleb, alone in his empty shack, refused to believe his Lucy Jane, the woman of his dreams, was just imaginary. For her portrait sat above the mantle, looking down – her whisper smile, her raven hair, her skin so soft and white – keeping company every minute of every hour of every day the cold and lonely echo of his heart.

But there were nights when the autumn wind blew harsh, reminding Caleb of winter's coming, when he wondered what would happen if he should take the portrait of his Lucy Jane down from its mantelpiece and place it in the woodstove flames.

Would her loveliness return in all its living color? Or would she be lost forever?

It was a choice he hoped he'd never have to make.

II. Julia

Julia, daughter of Lucy Jane, born from ash and oil colors, a second-generation portrait painted by the lover of her mother's fading memory.

Her creator, Caleb John, had tried to survive the long, cold winter in the pines, her mother's portrait by his side, but it grew too frigid to keep. And so, one night, he was forced to toss the portrait in the dying winter fire.

So beautiful the colors that danced within the feathered heat. Caleb could only watch as phantom smiles and jewel-lit eyes, once captured, now released, escaped into the crystal night. But the warmth he felt upon his skin could not be felt as deeply within his heart, because he knew this night would be the last his eyes would fall upon his love's reflection.

The following morning, winter broke and warmer weather shined, as if to rub the cold and lifeless ashes of Lucy Jane's memory into his lonely open wound. But when he stepped outside the pinewood shack into the melting snow, he knelt and nearly cried.

Upon each sunlit tree, upon each needled bough, he saw the glint of phantom smiles and the wink of jewel-lit eyes. The pines, once green and dull, appeared as if painted by the spirit of one who was once so colorful.

It was then that Caleb, his artist's need reborn, retrieved the ashes from the portrait fire and set about mixing oils and pigments. If he had created one, perhaps he could create another, one just as beautiful, with raven hair, a whisper smile and skin so soft and white. He let the beauty captured in the pines provide the inspiration for his art.

Once complete, the face that gazed at Caleb from the canvas stretched within the portrait frame was slightly different than the last. A daughter, perhaps?

After staring long upon the portrait born of ash and oil, painted with the same love that created her now pine-tree-bound mother, Caleb found a name as soft and beautiful as Lucy Jane, one that would stay forever bound within his heart. And that name was Julia.

It was then a loud and clumsy noise echoed from inside the empty shack, and Caleb, standing ankle deep in melting snow, felt a chill run up his spine. For the noise was not the delicate movement of a woman sprucing up a woodland home or preparing a morning meal, but the desperate sounds of an animal trapped and looking for escape.

When Caleb gained the nerve, at last, to open up the door, a wolf, as long and slender as a woman on all fours and silver as the moonlight that brushed the pines at night, bolted from the shack. It knocked his artist's easel to the ground and into the woods it fled without a backward glance.

The portrait of Julia, still wet and now wetter still, ran into the melting snow, until the canvas was a smear of colors resembling more a bleeding sunset, or a creature fleeting through the forest, than the portrait of a love created to warm the heart of a cold and lonely man.

And so Caleb, his artist's pride bruised but not broken, salvaged what he could, and with a new canvas stretched across the portrait frame, and an image in his mind of something distant but something likely there all along, began what he had hoped would be his final portrait.

III. Caleb John

Throughout the day into the dusk, Caleb John, his ankles deep in melting snow, painted with a flourish.

Fingernails, clipped and ground, locks of hair he no longer needed to warm his scalp –each was added to a smoldering char to form a paste. He mixed it all with oil colors recovered from his previous portrait, a captured vision of a woman by the name of Julia, who escaped into the wild in the sleek and fleeting form of a silver wolf, herself a vision conjured from the smoke and ash remains of his love's reflection, Lucy Jane.

To the music-drip of icicles he stroked the canvas, blending shapes and lending shadow, rending phantom memories and the smoke-like fancies that once warmed his cold and lonely heart.

For the first time in his life, he saw himself no longer just a drab and lifeless spectator among the tall and watchful pines. With Lucy Jane alight in every needle of every bough, and Julia the silver twine that ran between them, he placed himself inside the colors that bled from his inspired yet tired fingertips, and instead of painting the world as he saw it, he painted the world for which he yearned, a world he hoped, in turn, would accept him unconditionally.

And as the sun sank low into the pines with a beauty and grace only witnessed when no eyes are there to see, Caleb John, full of want but no longer wretched in need, lost in his artist's spell, began to slowly bleed into the landscape.

TIME AFTER TIME

by
Morgan Elektra

"First of all, before you say it – *not* like a cat. It's happened more than nine…"

My throat goes dry. I sip my water, the glass cool against my sweaty palms. David watches me, brows drawn down over his nose. I am unable to steal my gaze from his face.

"Honestly, I don't even know how many times it's happened anymore."

"*Chris.*" He says my name like I hit him. "What do you mean 'before I say it'?"

He was already thinking it; I can tell by the way he bites his lip. I drink in the sight, more satisfying than the flat water. Filling some part of me that belongs only to him.

I've tried to stay away, but the worst happened anyway and I missed the chance to kiss him. I won't do that again.

Maybe this is hell. Didn't someone famous once say 'Hell is repetition'? Except my world is constantly changing. Britain won the Revolution, religion is as taboo as kinky sex, the Cold War is still on. Or never happened. Or hasn't started yet.

I'm always me, though. And no matter what David is – writer, soldier, politician or pauper – he's always him, too. Same scar under his lip and kind hazel eyes, though there are more lines around them than there used to be.

Which makes me think it must be real.

The noise of the diner presses in on me; the clatter of dishes, the low murmur of patrons.

It feels so familiar, though I've never been *here* before.

Suddenly, the ticking of the clock on the wall drowns out everything. I can feel time slipping away, like trying to hold water in my fist. David stares at me, and I realize I haven't answered his question.

"You always say it. I say, '*I keep coming back*,' and you say, '*Like a cat?*' I know it sounds crazy, but if you'll just *listen*."

He ducks his head in a quick nod, a lock of nearly black hair falling over his forehead. I lean over and push it back.

"I'll be quick," I say. And then I laugh, even though I don't mean to. Because it seems like all I've got is time.

All the time in the world and yet never enough.

I catch a whiff of the soap he uses. It's minty, with a hint of cedar. No matter where I find him – arctic or tropics, rich or poor – he always smells like this. It eases me.

So, I tell him about the first time I died, outside the movie theater in twenty twelve.

I can still hear the soft patter of the rain on my umbrella, audible even over Modern English crooning "Melt With You" in my earbuds.

The smell of the air, that dusty wet pavement scent mixed with ozone, seems to linger in my lungs even all these lifetimes later.

David stood under the marquee, grinning. His hair was wet, gleaming in the streetlight like seal skin.

The bullet wasn't intended for me, I don't think. It was just a 'wrong place, wrong time' situation. It always is.

The shot was a punch to the center of my back. I lost my breath. And his eyes…

God, his *eyes*.

I knew it was bad before I saw the blood. Bright red, spattered all across the pale wool of his sweater.

His voice broke on my name. I focused on the smell of him, the feel of his mouth on mine, warm against my chilled skin. Rain fell in my eyes, but I fought to keep them open.

It didn't work.

It never does.

Eventually, they close and I'm back in the darkness, surrounded by nothing. No sight. No sound. No *anything* but the faintly disorienting sense of hurtling forward into the black. And then they open again, on a different time. A different place. A different world.

And then we find each other.

"And then I die again."

The diner is empty now. The busboy sits at

the counter, arguing with the cook over a baseball game – the New York Knickerbockers versus the Atlanta Gators. The waitress refills salt shakers; I can hear the sibilant cascade of the grains.

David reaches for his coffee. His hands tremble. "Do you know when it's going to happen?"

He always asks this too.

He's pale, his five-o'clock shadow standing out stark on his cheeks.

I shake my head. "I never know. Sometimes, I get a week. A few months. We got two years once, in Mexico. It was…" I sigh, breathing out a mist of warm memories. "*Lovely*."

We found each other quickly that time, and he bought me a cup of dark, strong coffee and told me he felt like he knew me before I even told him about the skipping.

Now, I tie the flimsy straw wrapper into knots.

He plucks it from my fingers. "Skipping?"

"I don't know the hows or whys. Alternate dimensions. Parallel realities. Time travel." I shrug, mouth tipping sideways. "That's more your thing than mine. But… it feels like I'm a stone. Someone plucked me from the water and skipped me across a very big lake. Mostly, I'm whipping through the air while the world passes by below me. And I'm always flying forward, but the water… it ebbs and flows."

I pause, because I can never think exactly how to convey that I am traveling in a straight line, but everything around me is always shifting.

"I touch the world – briefly – and then I'm back in the air."

I flick my fingers out towards the brightening sky beyond the wide front windows and get momentarily lost in the thin edge of shimmering pearl above the treeline, pushing back the dark blue velvet of night.

The incessant ticking of the clock on the wall makes more words tumble from my lips.

"England, *skip*, Ireland, *skip*, France, *skip*, Portugal… even the Canadian wilderness once. God, it was cold! Nineteen twelve, eighteen sixteen, twelve eighty-six, twenty thirty-three, oh one oh seven oh three oh…"

His eyes get wider and wider. I run out of breath before I run out of numbers and I see the belief recede a little.

"And now. *Now*."

He lets me take his hands and I squeeze them hard, until my knuckles turn white.

I'm not explaining it well. Some times are harder than others.

He never remembers. Each time we meet, it's new to him. But I remember *everything*. Every minute. Every world. Every life.

Every single mortal wound.

My death is always in his future. Yet it's been at least a decade since I first listened to him begging me to stay while his tears mixed with the rain.

Occasionally, all those years get tangled up on my tongue.

"Hey." He cups my cheek. The warmth of his palm settles around my heart and I breathe easier. He nods. "We'll figure this out. Stones don't skip forever."

Everything goes still. That feeling of moving forward too fast to breathe just… stops.

I blink. My mouth opens, but I close it again because there aren't any words waiting to come out.

His chuckle is raspy and a faint pink blush stains his cheeks. "What? Do I say that all the time too?"

A forgotten joy, so fierce it burns, radiates through my body like the first rays of sun breaking over the horizon.

"Never," I croak.

He's *never* said it. I didn't think there was anything left that he'd never said.

His hand in mine is warm and steady. Maybe this time, I can hold on.

A slim, ruddy youth slouches in from the empty parking lot and heads for the counter, hands in his pockets, calling the waitress' name. The jaunty tinkle of the bell over the door makes me grin. The answering curve of David's mouth sends my heart thumping hard against my ribs.

I feel like I'm falling. I don't realize I've said

so until he speaks.

"Don't worry, I'll catch you," he whispers.

I start to reply, but the words get stuck in my throat, thick as molasses, burnt and bitter. Because David's not looking at me anymore, he's looking over my shoulder. At the youth at the counter. And I see it in his eyes.

This isn't the time I stay.

The waitress' screams don't drown out the sound of the gun cocking, but I tune it out. All I can hear is what David said about stones.

It can't go on forever. One day, I'll sink back into the cool, soothing depths of the water for good. One day, I won't have to go.

"I'll be waiting." I manage to get the words out past numb lips.

There's no punch this time. No pain. No bright splatter of blood. Just the feel of his hand in mine, that lovely, dear face… and then darkness.

Skip.

BONUS STORY: ENLIGHTENMENT ADRIFT

by
Steven Rooke

1

The Corsair Rogue scythed through the swelling sea, angry tides battering its sleek hull. Ghostdragon Lily steadied herself on the gunwale as the swift pirate galleon soared towards a lurching hulk that drifted darkly on the twilight horizon.

Lily raised her brass spyglass and peered at their prey. It was listing on the waves, its sails tattered rags hanging from rotting masts, its hull cracked and battered by the tempestuous Monocore Sea.

"She looks a derelict," said Lily, handing the spyglass to the rainbow elf beside her. "A merchantman, triple-master. A big hold. She's been adrift for many years, I'll warrant, for she rots like a corpse in a tidal cage. She could not make sail with those rags and her timbers are as perished as her canvas. What say you?"

The elf took the spyglass from her gingerly. That he must touch a spyglass that the boneskin had touched repulsed him. Had they been in the Rainbow Empire, Ghostdragon Lily would have been branded and kept on a chain. Humans would never be permitted to touch such tools of cultured learning, much less female humans.

Careful not to let the instrument touch the skin around his eye, Purity observed the dark merchantman through the spyglass. "It is a Cantor ship, by the Casatan runes on her bow. She is named Enlightenment."

"And what is a Cantor ship?"

He handed the spyglass back to her. "The Cantors are the Custodians of the Songs of Symmetry, the singers of the Canticle."

"And what is the Canticle? Let's pretend I care."

Purity looked down at Lily's freckled face, framed in locks of burnt orange that hid the hideous roundness of her ears. The freckles clung to her like a pox, ruining the flawless, pure, exquisite thing that skin should be.

"The Canticle is the song that tells the tale of the Rainbow Empire," Purity told her proudly, "from its rise at the time of the Unification to what will be its eventual conquest of all things and the subsequent ordering of the world into divine symmetry. The Cantors record the tale in their songs."

"I thought that was the Symmetry Guard?"

"The Symmetry Guard are the military arm of the Cantors." He swung his gaze back to the drifting ship so he would not have to further suffer her offensively asymmetric aspect, her left eye being at least the breadth of a swamp fly bigger than her right. "Long have I yearned to hear the songs of the Cantors again. They are very beautiful."

"I'll make sure to cry for you," grinned Lily. "Crow! In boarding her, I'll not lose my pretty face to a light spear. What see you?"

"Naught but rotten timbers thick with sea mould," called the crow from his nest. "She is long since abandoned, Captain. None walk its decks save ghosts."

"There is certainly a stench of decay about her." Lily touched her eyelids and teeth in silent prayer to whatever heathen gods she worshipped.

"And death," Purity said slowly, sniffing the air. "There are corpses aboard."

"Unsunk dead? Then spirits stalk her decks, I'll warrant. Or are the Cantors the kind to lay ambush in this way?"

"I think not," scoffed Purity. "With light spears, they have no need of ambush."

"Mayhap. By its condition, the ship is long since abandoned. Many years, I'll warrant. It is a wonder no storm has sunk it or broken it upon rocks. What need have the Cantors for a ship anyway? To where do they sail?"

Purity sneered. The ship's purpose was clear as a three sun dawn in the words painted on her bow. But Casatan was a beautiful language, a divine language, the language of the Empire, a language that Lily's coarse human tongue could never hope to comprehend.

"She is a mission ship."

"They seek converts to their bloody cause?" Lily laughed. "Bound for Port Heliotrope, are they?"

"Do not jest of the Cantors," he warned with a glare. "They are the purest of the pure. And they would not suffer to send a mission ship to the city of the damned and the lost."

"I should think not. We would butcher them."

"They would send a fleet instead," Purity snapped. "Mighty of bow and sail and laden with warriors. They would raze the port with fire and sword so that no stone remained upon stone and no head upon shoulders."

"So, whither in the name of the kingless are they bound?"

"The Cantor missions seek converts in the Floating Cities and among the fire elves of the Mercantile Protectorate and the Slave Coast Palatinate."

"So they will be carrying gifts with which to bribe converts?" Lily's eyes flared. "What might we find on board as a little bonus? Spills of cotton yarn? Rolls of damask? Articles of white steel? A gold-stitched tome or two?"

"I know not, but I have paid you well enough not to loot a Cantor ship, even a derelict one."

Iron hooks were cast upon the derelict's gunwale. Timbers creaked and some broke under the pull of the grapples, but they were cast again until secure. The Rogue's anchor plunged into the choppy sea and held both vessels steady.

The vast, forbidding ship towered over the pirate vessel. The sky darkened as the last of the suns set. The sea had become more turbulent the moment they had pulled alongside the hulk.

Cold, unseen fingers seemed to reach out from the vessel and claw at Purity's skin. "I board her alone."

"I think not," hissed Lily, leaning uncomfortably close. "Should you be lost, my voyage would have been for naught and I would have a very angry crew to pay and not so much as a Republican florin with which to pay them."

"They will loot the ship like the animals they are."

"Of course they will, but you trust me, don't you, Purity? Let me come aboard and I'll ensure the rest stay on the Rogue. You know how reliable I am. My word is my bond."

Her smile taunted him, but he needed her ship, her damnable, filthy, infested ship.

The Castellan of Heliotrope had taken a relatively small bribe to release the Rogue from dock after confiscating it for Lily's little indiscretion. She still maintained that she had no idea how that crystal ivory had accidentally slipped inside those barrels of potash just before excise boarded them at the South Harbour.

Nonetheless, Purity offered her seven storm sapphires for this voyage, or five if he could not find what he was looking for – kalkyte spears for his spearcaster, the devastating weapon that had made the Rainbow Empire superior to all others.

"No human shall defile that ship with their presence. They are all filthy, vile, asymmetric things."

"I should keep such thoughts to myself if I were you," warned Lily. "You may pay handsomely for this trip, but some of the crew might take offence even so and try for your back with their blades."

Purity glanced over his shoulder at the human crew, men and a few women, boneskins, darklings and cinnamons, flawed and ugly and asymmetric. They glowered at him, sizing him up.

"Besides," whispered Lily, "I'm sure you don't include me in that. Not sweet little beautiful Ghostdragon Lily."

Purity glared. None knew exactly how proficient Lily was with the ghostdragon hex, nor how much she simply bluffed. Fate had slaughtered more than a few of her enemies in uncanny ways and it was fear of such curses cast for unpaid debts that had compelled some to crew the Rogue on this voyage.

"Just you," he growled.

2

Purity dropped over the gunwale of the Enlightenment, his white steel scimitar in his fist. The timbers creaked and cracked beneath him. He swung his iron lantern to and fro, casting the gloom from decomposing timbers, putrefying masts, tattered sails and flailing rigging. His eyes skimmed amidships, across the capstan and the rusty chains that secured the hatches, the aft where the battered wheel rolled lazily and the forecastle, beneath which mouldy doors sealed the dark depths of the ship.

"Are you dead?" called Ghostdragon Lily.

"No," said Purity flatly.

"Then I'll come aboard." She dropped down beside him, a lantern in one hand, a long, slender sword in the other. "Alone at last," she smiled.

"I seek not your company."

"I'm devastated." She glanced around nervously. "Quiet, is it not?"

They were sixteen days out from Port Heliotrope on a fair leeward wind, as close to the lands of the Rainbow Empire as a respectable businesswoman dare go without fear of running into an Oyster Islands storm chaser or a sea elf privateer. Or a horde of heavily armed rainbow elves seeking slaughter and slaves.

Lily shuddered. She kicked at the rusted chains that secured the hatches, but the grimy padlocks held.

"They may take some time to break," she said. "Needs must we enter the hold by the forecastle doors. I do not wish to tarry long aboard her."

Purity stopped her with the flat of his blade.

Lily smiled disarmingly. "What you seek is in the hold, I'll warrant."

"Loot her and I shall slay you," he said simply.

"Of course," she said sweetly. "You know you can trust me."

She watched him cross to the forecastle, his hair many colours, smooth and soft, his face so strong and hard and so very beautiful. He was tall and he had that strange grace that all elves had, an elegance in every movement that made every other race look clumsy. Every now and then, Ghostdragon Lily lusted after Purity's body, usually when she was drunk on rotgut.

But she did not like his skin. It was so smooth and unblemished, so perfect, as if he were a painted portrait rather than flesh and blood. It made him appear unreal, out of focus, a ghost at once beautiful to behold, yet distant and untouchable, a fantasy of what living things should be, lacking the imperfection of the truly perfect.

Except for the scar on his cheek. It was small, barely a couple of inches. She had worse scars on her back from her spell in the Knight Emperor's penal legion. But Purity's scar was imperfection. Imperfection meant an elf must slay himself in line with the doctrines of the Rainbow Empire. Purity had instead chosen exile and was thus called abomination by his own people, an unholy traitor to the Gods of Order.

The forecastle doors creaked open on rusty hinges and the stench of death belched up from the depths of the ship. Lily recoiled, but Purity plunged into the darkness, clambering down wooden steps and casting the halo of his lantern about the vast hold.

"Are you dead?" Lily called from above.

"Yes."

Lily descended the decaying steps and moved up beside the elf. Her stomach turned over. In the twin glow of their lanterns, the Enlightenment's grisly cargo festered. Corpses carpeted the hold, hundreds of them packed in tight. Their eyes were empty, their faces petrified, mouths wide with horror, mould and filth crusting decomposing skin stretched tight over ridged bones. They were clothed only in tattered grey rags and every one of them was manacled by their wrists and ankles.

"Purity?" breathed Lily, her gaze horribly locked. "These are rainbow elves."

"Not all," he spat, hatred thickening his voice. "Some are the Tainted."

"The Tainted?"

"Half-men." He fairly vomited the words. "Debased creatures with no place in the Great Order."

"You mean half-elves?" realised Lily.

"I mean half-men!" he snapped. "It is their human blood that perverts them, that ruins the natural perfection of the elves, that gives them hair upon their chins and lips, that rounds their ears and makes crooked their faces and their bodies. Such things can only come from human contamination."

"I never realised I was so special," murmured Lily.

"Elves must be pure, else we betray the Gods of Order and acquiesce to chaos of form."

"But how came these half-elves to be if mating with humans is forbidden?"

"Half-men," Purity growled.

"If you like."

"Many fled east to sanctuary in Kyrya and Pharok when the Rainbow Emperor ascended. The Empire must have taken those lands now. That means the war must be going very well, for the Empire to have advanced so far so quickly. Such is the awesome might of the Rainbow!"

There was triumph in his voice and he was smiling. He hardly ever smiled, yet this pile of shackled corpses had made him happy.

Anger lurched through Lily. It was rare that she was angry, unless there was profit in it. She had seen death of course, but never in such quantity, and quantity was proving so much more disturbing than quality. And the shackles, the shackles incensed her, for she had known such shackles in Staltarg, known the helplessness and the fear and the impotence, the knowledge that when pain and death came she could not run, nor fight, but only be a helpless plaything for any who wished to indulge their sadistic pleasures.

"You think this is wonderful," she stated coldly.

"Of course!" he cried, excited as a child with a honey cake. "Kyrya and Pharok must now be pure. Symmetry has been given to them. They have found Enlightenment. They are once more under the aegis of the Gods of Order. When the Canticle is finished, when Enlightenment reaches all the lands of the world, then we shall have the Great Order in all things, just as the Gods decree. Chaos shall be vanquished, there shall be no disorder, no creatures that do not fit the perfection of form that is the elf, only peace and harmony and blissful communion with the Gods for all eternity. Orcs shall be unknown, their foulness wiped from the world. Ogres shall be gone, yes, and dwarfs too and all those other foul things that are spawned of chaos, that bring anarchy to form and life."

"And humans?"

"Yes," he said. "If they do not acquiesce to Enlightenment."

"You mean become slaves."

"That is the only place that humans can have in the Great Order."

Her eyes narrowed. A smile teased the corners of her mouth. "You really believe in the Great Order, don't you?"

He frowned, wondering why she should need to ask such a question. "It is divine."

"You believe in everything that the Rainbow believes in?"

"Of course! We are one. We are perfection."

"Then why do you not slay yourself, for you are abomination?"

Purity's fingers shot to the scar on his cheek. He snatched his eyes away from her. "Do not speak of things that you do not understand!"

"No answer," she snarled. "There is no answer, Purity, like there is no reason for this. Half-elves some may be, but not all. Some look like you, Purity. What then is their crime against the Great Order?"

"Look there upon the brands on their foreheads." He swung the lantern out across the hold. "You can still see the hexagons on their rotting flesh. They are he-elves who have lain with other he-elves."

"And that is a crime?"

"Of course!" he cried incredulously. "There is a perfect order to all things, a divine order. That order has created two perfect creatures in he-elves and she-elves and together, their union forms communion with and worship of the Gods of Order. There is no place in the divine order for those who would lay with their own sex, for that is an unholy union, a devastation of divine order, a murder of harmony, the mark of the Gods of Chaos. It is not natural!"

"Good fun, though."

"I expect such things from an ugly race like yours," Purity scoffed. "Ugly of form, ugly of soul. So asymmetric!"

"I'm so humbled," Lily sneered, pulse racing, fists tight, a tempest in her skull. "Tell me, then, O Great One, where were they taking these unfortunates? Not to the Protectorate or the Palatinate, I'll warrant. And if they are so abhorrent to the Rainbow, why go to the expense of transporting them? Why not just slaughter them?"

"I confess I know not wither this ship be bound," Purity admitted irritably. "Nor does it serve my purpose to know, any more than this hold is likely to store what I seek. Weapons would not be stowed with prisoners. I shall search out the captain's cabin."

Purity whirled about and ascended the creaking stairs as Lily called, "Purity, if we had a child, would they end their days here?"

"We shall never have a child!" he snapped.

"I could get you drunk," grinned Lily, "and have my wicked way with you when you are barely conscious."

"I would slay you before your vile flesh could defile mine."

She laughed, loud and mocking.

Purity slammed the mouldy door behind him.

"What a charming fellow," Lily muttered and sighed jaggedly, her eyes drawn inexorably back to the mass grave of the hold.

She knew the Rainbow slaughtered en masse. That was why thousands of refugees fled to Heliotrope. Wars claimed far more lives than the few hundred corpses in this hold. Bandit warlords murdered and pillaged their way through entire cities. Slavery was rife in all the lands of the world. Brutality was life. And yet this scene of carnage disturbed her, angered her, made her feel sick.

"It's just the first time you've seen so many dead in one place," she told herself, trying to control her breathing. "Just think of the money you're earning, those lovely, valuable, rare storm sapphires, lovely things, and everything will be alright."

She swung her lantern across the hold, peering at the carcasses in the ghostly luminescence.

"I'll warrant they've stripped you lot of anything that might swell the coffers of a respectable business woman."

Then something caught her eye, a rich cerise drowned in scarlet upon a grey palm. She picked her way gingerly among the dead and flung the lantern over the upturned hand of a half-elf cadaver. Her heart thumped a savage beat in her breast. It was a piece of pink coral, drenched in the crusted blood of the prisoner.

Lily knew of such things. She knew blood drenching certain substances was reputed to curse enemies or even… summon… things…

Suddenly, the darkness screeched.

Lily jolted about, swinging the lantern across the hold. She tightened her grip on the sword and strained her eyes into the gloom.

"Who's there?" she called across the rotting sea of corpses. "Is someone still alive?"

The lantern flared across the timber hull, casting a spectral glow upon a bundle of tattered rags. The bundle shuddered and there was a scraping, as if of a steel blade against a whetstone.

Lily opened her mouth to cry out for Purity, but no sound came. She tried to close her mouth but could not bring her lips together. Her face froze. Her eyelids locked open.

The bundle of rags lifted a gnarled claw. In it was a mask carved out of jade coral from the sea floor, a mask that somehow, in some monstrous, accursed way, resembled Lily's face. The eyes were open and the mouth was wide, frozen in a scream of terror.

Lily's heart shrieked in her chest, but no sound escaped her lips. Her lantern flickered out and plunged the hold into darkness.

3

Purity strode along the lurching ship and burst into the rotting ruins of the captain's cabin. He found the captain's log on a narrow table infested with sea worm. He hauled open the blue leather tome and rifled through yellowed pages. They crumbled at his touch, scattering to dust. He slowed, anxious not to destroy any more records. He reached the log's final entry painted in Casatan, the elegant script formed of perfectly symmetrical runes. They made Purity ache for Penacasata, the glittering capital of the Rainbow Empire.

Suddenly, his eyes flared. The captain's last entry reported all being well on the voyage of the Enlightenment. The entry was dated in the Rainbow Calendar. There could be no question. The last entry was but two days ago.

A great clamour burst upon the ship. He snatched up his lantern and flung himself from the cabin.

The cries wailed from the Corsair Rogue, the pirates pointing, yelling. The grappling lines snapped along the length of the gunwale, their fibres rotted in but minutes of contact with the Cantor ship. The last rope burst in a flower of dusty hemp and the Enlightenment lurched away from the Rogue on the churning black sea.

"Bring her back alongside!" roared Purity, flinging himself against the gunwale.

The pirates stared in fright or touched their eyes and teeth or screeched prayers and curses to their heathen gods.

"I'll double your pay!" yelled Purity across the yawning chasm wrenched between the two ships.

The crew scrambled about the deck of the Rogue. Her sail unfurled. Whether they were doing as he demanded or setting sail for Heliotrope with all haste, Purity could not tell.

He cupped his hands around his mouth and hollered, "Remember the ghostdragon hex!"

If they heard, he did not know.

He scrambled along the tilting deck to the padlocked hatches. "Lily! Needs must we go now! This ship is cursed!"

Something moved on the forecastle.

Purity shot his gaze upon the unmistakable symmetry of a he-elf. It stood still and silent despite the lurching ship, its tattered black cloak flicking around its strong, perfect body, a violent wind tossing its hair about its strangely still face. The elf seemed to be smiling at him, a crooked smile, broad and fixed, like that of the tricksters of the theatre or the Laughing God of the sea elves.

"Cantor!" Purity called, uncertain if he was deceived by a ghostly illusion. "I am a rainbow elf, a Warlord of the Fenris."

The Cantor raised his spearcaster.

Purity dropped the lantern and flung himself to the deck. The spear burst forth in a bolt of searing blue light, smashing a hole through the gunwale and fizzing into the churning sea in a cloud of steam. Purity rolled and flung himself behind the capstan. He glanced out, seeing the Cantor locking another spear into the caster.

That was time enough.

Purity drew daggers from his coat, sprang up and flung them at the Cantor. They caught the elf in the shoulder and the neck. He jolted and gurgled, but the grin remained. Ignorant of the blades that skewered his flesh, the Cantor raised the caster. Purity spun aside as light flashed hot and tore the central mast in two. With a roar it toppled forwards, shattering timbers and ploughing into the lower decks.

Purity's scimitar rasped from its sheath, and he sprang upon the forecastle. The Cantor reloaded his caster. Purity swung. Scarlet splashed white steel.

Partially severed, the Cantor's head still clung to his shoulders, the mocking smile crooked and bloody. The Cantor raised the caster. Purity kicked him in the guts. The Cantor fell and his shot went skyward, a shooting star in the dark. Purity crashed the scimitar upon the elf's upturned face. There was a glitter of coral dust and a crunch of bone. The Cantor lay lifeless upon the deck.

Purity glanced around for more assailants. He saw none.

"Forgive me, Cantor," he breathed solemnly. "I slew you not as a rainbow elf, but as a pawn of witchery."

The cloven smile was a mask carved from turquoise coral in mockery of elven beauty. It was nailed to the Cantor's face.

"Mask magic," Purity hissed, for he had heard many tales of such things from the sea elves when he was a child, before the war, before the ships stopped coming and the ports fell silent.

He looted the Cantor's caster and remaining kalkyte spears. He loaded the caster, clambered down amidships, snatched up his lantern and kicked open the forecastle door.

"Lily!" he yelled into the gloom. "We must be away. Come hither now!"

Silence.

"Lily! Curse you, Lily! We must be away. There is a haunting here. We must go."

Darkness.

"I'll leave you here, Lily. I'll take the Rogue. I'll leave you behind to rot and drown."

Nothing.

"Curse you, Lily," he whispered.

He descended the creaking, cracking steps into the bowels of the haunted ship. He swept the lantern across the murky hold, across the grisly corpses, the rusting shackles and the festering timbers. Shadows scattered and fled before the light, and Purity caught a flash of fiery orange in the gloom.

"Lily! We must away!"

Lily was sitting with her back against the hull, her knees up, her arms limp by her side, her mouth open, her eyes wide and staring, her freckled face frozen in fright.

"Sea hag," Purity snarled through gritted teeth.

On the edge of his vision, Purity glimpsed an image slashed from sinister shades. It was a bundle of black rags. The bundle moved, a gnarled claw rising from the tattered robes. It clutched a jade coral mask in its bony fingers, a mask of Lily's face frozen in terror.

The creature looked up from beneath its cowl and the hideous visage twisted into the light of Purity's lantern. Its eyes were black, hollow sockets sunk in a cadaverous face, worms writhing in cracked skin stretched taut over a ridged skull. The nose was hooked and thick with sea mould. In its black gaping maw, razored teeth dripped slimy venom that hissed as it seared the deck.

Purity could tolerate the repulsive orcs and the repugnant trolls, the ratlings, ogres, boglings and goblins, even the bulgs and the fetch. But such was the hideousness of the sea hag that he tore his face away and retched.

The sea hag gurgled with what might have been pleasure. Then, as Purity forced his eyes back to the creature, it shoved the coral mask onto Lily's frozen face.

The sea hag brandished a rusty hammer and pushed the point of a long timber nail against the mask, just below Lily's right eye. Its lipless maw curled into a malignant smile.

Lily could not scream, kick, fight. She could not escape her hideous fate. She was motionless, impotent. Through the carved holes of the mask, her eyes burned with violent terror. The hammer swung.

Purity blasted the sea hag. His light spear rocketed through the creature and the hull and disappeared into the night. The long nail clattered to the deck.

The sea hag looked slowly down at the smoking hole in its guts. Then it raised its putrescent head and smirked.

Purity almost vomited again.

He ripped his eyes away and locked another spear into the caster. He raised it as the sea hag picked the long nail off the deck and pushed the point against Lily's death mask.

"Do not do this, sea hag!" he snarled.

The sea hag raised the rusty hammer. Lily's eyes flamed with frenzied fear.

Purity lowered the spearcaster and shot at Ghostdragon Lily. The deck by her feet shattered. The rotten timbers collapsed under her and Lily plummeted into the bilges. The mask dropped from her face and splashed into the filthy water beside her. She lay on her back, still frozen, staring up through the hole in the deck at the faint flicker of lantern light that dared battle the ravenous darkness.

The sea hag gurgled as if it was choking on blood. It pulled a rusty knife and a large piece of ochre coral from its ragged robes. As Purity locked another spear into the caster the sea hag scraped the knife across the coral with a violent screech.

Purity felt his cheeks start to freeze, his jaw start to lock, his blood start to turn cold in his veins.

He pointed the caster at the mask the sea hag was carving, but his hands stiffened. His trigger finger locked as his eyes wedged open. He tried to squeeze the trigger, tried to fire the spear, but he could not.

Fear crushed his heart in a bony fist.

The sea hag carved swiftly, crafting an elven face that grinned like a madcap. Purity's lips curled into an unnatural, insane smile.

All he could now see was the hag, an atrocity of form. Such detestable mayhem of shape had no right to live. It had murdered the beauty and perfection of the Cantors, the exalted symmetry of the elves.

He thought of the Rainbow Empire, of that divine, blissful, exquisite realm that would never welcome its Cantors home, of his exile from it, of the unhappy chance that had made him abomination, of the horrors he had had to endure in the world outside the Empire, of all the terrible ugliness he had had to suffer to exist, of Port Heliotrope, the city of the damned and the lost, his home in exile, infested with all the ugly, evil, unholy races of the world. He hated them, hated them. Hated every single one of the hateful, hateful things.

Hatred slammed the trigger.

The coral mask exploded. The sea hag shrieked.

Every muscle in Purity's body flexed free. He swept a spear from his belt and locked it. He fired at the deck beneath the shrieking monster.

The sea hag plummeted into the bilges. Purity sprang to the edge of the hole in the deck and loaded his last spear. As the sea hag rose from the filthy water and hissed up at him with rage he fired his spear at its feet. The hull shattered beneath it, and the hag plunged into the churning sea, sinking into the black depths from which it had been summoned.

Water rushed into the ship.

Purity leapt into the bilges, found the jade coral mask and shattered it with his scimitar.

Lily shuddered, snapped her eyes shut, blinked and stared up at the rainbow elf. "It's about time." She held out a hand for him to haul her up.

"The ship is sinking," said Purity, not wishing to defile himself. "And the Corsair Rogue is not alongside. Let us hope your crew have not abandoned you."

"They would not dare." Lily jumped to her feet, wishing she could stop shaking.

Suddenly, the rotting hull gave way in a dozen places. Water surged in.

"She's breaking up!"

They half-waded, half-swam to a ladder, clambered up the buckling rungs to the hold and then up the crumbling steps and through the mouldy door to the deck. They flung themselves against the gunwale, and their hearts soared as they saw the Corsair Rogue rushing upon them at full sail. Fear of the ghostdragon hex had saved Lily once more.

They were cast from their feet as the ship lurched to one side, then the other in its wild death throes, and Lily laughed, looking up at the black sky through drenched locks. Then she wanted to cry.

Instead, she just screamed at Purity, "What in the name of the kingless was that?!"

"A sea hag," said Purity, trying to regain his feet. "A horror of the deeps. I heard tales of them in Anacallista when I was young. It slaughtered everyone aboard and rotted the ship."

Lily staggered up against the gunwale, gripping the tattered rigging. "It was summoned by one of the half-elves. He probably hoped it could save him."

"Save him?!" snorted Purity. "A sea hag? They are puppeteers of the soul. Why should such a creature save him? How pathetic these half-men are. Their brains are addled by human blood."

"He was terrified out of his mind because he was shackled in the bowels of a slave ship. He was desperate."

"He was a halfwit," spat Purity.

The ship rocked and cast them from their feet. They staggered up.

Purity glanced at Lily and his gaze locked for a moment.

Lily's spider silk shirt and cotton breeches were wet through and clung to the curves of her body, sliding tight and contoured around her breasts and waist and hips and thighs. But she was not symmetrical like a she-elf, so she must be ugly.

Must be.

"I am not an elf."

"No," he agreed, tearing his eyes away and cursing himself. "You are a human, ugly and asymmetric."

"That's the tragedy of my existence. Now about my fee…"

"Five storm sapphires only. I found spears but used them all against the sea hag."

"That's not my problem. We agreed seven if you found spears. You could have used them on anything you wished. It was your choice to use them to save my pretty face."

"You are captain of the Corsair Rogue," Purity growled. "If you did not return to the ship with me, your crew would as likely stab me in the back as deliver me safely to Heliotrope. I saved you only because I had to."

"That's not the only reason, I'll warrant. You just did not want the sea hag to spoil my beauty by nailing that mask to my face."

"Do not deceive yourself! You can never be a she-elf. You shall never have such beauty, such perfection, no matter how much you may desire it."

"I do not need to have such perfection," Lily grinned, "for it is clear you desire me for what I am, a woman."

"You jest," Purity scoffed. "Women are ugly and that means they are evil. You saw the sea hag. It was ugly and it was evil. All evil things are ugly and therefore all ugly things must be evil. That is a universal truth, the ultimate truth. You cannot deny it."

"Beauty is in the eye of the beholder, so the bronzites say," she mused wistfully.

"That is nonsense, human nonsense."

"Then why does the Rainbow keep humans as slaves? Not for labour, I'll warrant, if the number of half-elves in that hold are anything to go by."

"You speak blasphemy, Lily," he snarled through gritted teeth.

"Do the he-elves never indulge their passions?"

"Never!"

"Nor the she-elves?"

"Never!"

"So there is no possibility that those half-elves came from little indiscretions with slaves?"

"None," he growled.

Lily grinned. One day, she would dance too close to the crocodile, and it would grab her in its jaws. One day.

The Enlightenment lurched and rolled, and a great spray rushed over them.

The Rogue pulled alongside. Grappling irons clattered along the gunwale.

"You see, Lily? I was right. Your crew would follow you across the Thirteen Oceans to the very corners of the world. You have a hold over them that I do not. That is the only reason I saved you. But have no doubts, this shall be our last voyage together. There are plenty of other ships for hire in Heliotrope. I shall not use yours again."

"Woe is me," she said, catching a rope swung across from the Rogue. "Seven storm sapphires, Purity. Remember what happens to those who mess with the ghostdragon hex."

She swung across to her ship. Purity slammed a fist against the rotting hulk. It splintered like hope in the dark.

"All ugliness is evil," he hissed. "Evil..."

Slowly, he raised a hand to the livid scar on his cheek.

"Or you can go down with the Enlightenment like a pious abomination should," taunted Lily from the deck of the Rogue.

He stared sadly across the gulf between the ships.

For a moment, Lily feared he would actually go down with the Enlightenment. For a moment, he looked small and helpless, a child lost in the great big world without friends or family or understanding. For a moment, she wanted him to release himself from his torment in the only way he could.

For a moment.

Then she mouthed a plea, forming the words in perfect Casatan, "Come home."

She swung him a rope. After all, she needed paying.

He caught the rope easily, elegantly. "The city of the damned and the lost," he whispered and abandoned the sinking ship.

ABOUT THE AUTHORS

TRAVIS BURNHAM

Travis Burnham is an SF&F writer and science teacher. His work has or will soon appear in *Far Fetched Fables*, *Hypnos Magazine*, *South85 Journal* and *Flash Fiction Online*. Originally from New England, he's lived in Japan, Colombia and the Mariana Islands and currently lives in Upstate South Carolina with his wife and pup. He's a bit of a thrill seeker, having bungee jumped in New Zealand, hiked portions of the Great Wall of China and gone scuba diving in Bali. He's got some novels looking for homes and can be found online at travisburnham.blogspot.com and travisburnhambooks.com.

JOHN A. MCCOLLEY

John A. McColley writes from the woods of New Hampshire, caught between millennia and a thousand shades and hues of reality. He's accompanied by his wonderfully creative wife, three small children, three cats and apparently this cricket. Despite all challenges to his writing time, he's turned out three novels in various stages of repair, published a few dozen SFFH short stories and become an associate member of the SFWA.

Find more from him at https://www.patreon.com/JohnAMcColley.

ANDREW BARRON

Andrew Barron is a writer and editor, who currently resides just outside Toronto, Ontario, Canada. During the daylight hours, he's an eCommerce professional, but he also has extensive journalistic writing and editing experience. Andrew is a prolific writer but sporadic submitter of his pieces. He loves to be scared by what he reads and watches, but he enjoys many genres – from true crime to horror to comedy and everything in between. Most of his free time is spent with his two young daughters, but he's also a long-suffering sports fan and dreams of championship parades for all his favourite teams.

RAJIV MOTÉ

Rajiv Moté is a writer living in Chicago with his wife, daughter and puppy. His stories make appearances in *Cast of Wonders*, *Diabolical Plots*, *Metaphorosis*, *McSweeney's Internet Tendency*, *Truancy* and others, and he has served as a slush-reading Badger for *Shimmer*. During the day, he gathers source material by masquerading as a software engineering manager. He scrapes off excess words on Twitter at @RajivMote and occasionally realizes he should put some effort into rajivmote.com.

MARIAH MONTOYA

Mariah Montoya is a writer from Idaho, the United States. Her work has been published in *Typehouse Literary Magazine, Luna Station Quarterly, Metaphorosis* and other journals. Her flash fiction piece "Moonpickers" was nominated for a Pushcart Prize by *Jersey Devil Press*. You can find Mariah on Instagram @mariah_author or <u>mariahmontoya.weebly.com</u>.

BRYAN MILLER

Bryan Miller is a writer and stand-up comedian based out of Minneapolis, Minnesota, USA. His horror stories have featured in *Intrinsick Magazine*, *Hellfire Crossroads* and *The Monsters We Forgot*. He's appeared on the CBS Late Late Show with Craig Ferguson, the Doug Loves Movies podcast and on Sirius/XM radio. He also writes about movies, American football, and opera.
You can find more from him at
<u>bryanmillercomedy.com</u>.

JEN SEXTON-RILEY

Jen Sexton-Riley is a speculative fiction writer. Born in rural New York, she found inspiration in a five-century-old sea goddess temple on the South China Sea and in the shadows of the world's southernmost subpolar forest. A Clarion West 2018 graduate, she proofreads an indie newspaper and lives by the sea with her husband and daughter. Her work has appeared in *Daily Science Fiction*, *The Colored Lens*, *Bewildering Stories*, and *Obscura: An Urban Fantasy Anthology*, edited by Corrugated Sky Publishing. Her work will appear in 2020 in *Ghostlight: The Magazine of Terror*, *Illumen*, *The Weird and Whatnot* and elsewhere.

You can find more from her at www.jensextonriley.com.

CHRISSIE ROHRMAN

Chrissie is a training supervisor who lives in Indianapolis, Indiana with her husband Zach and their five four-legged kiddos. She is currently drafting her debut novel "Fracture," the first installment of a Young Adult fantasy trilogy.

You can find more from her on Facebook (Chrissie Rohrman Writes Things) and Twitter (@ChrissieRawrman).

ALEXANDER LANGER

Alex Langer is a Canadian Jewish writer, law student and activist. He grew up in Toronto and now lives in Brooklyn, NY with his fiancée and cat. You can find his fiction elsewhere at *Aurelia Leo* (upcoming, July 2020), and his takes at @AlexLanger1993 on Twitter.

HAILEY PIPER

Hailey Piper is the author of *Benny Rose: The Cannibal King* from Unnerving and *An Invitation to Darkness* from Demain Publishing. Her short fiction appears in *Daily Science Fiction*, *The Bronzeville Bee*, *Tales to Terrify* and more. She lives in Maryland, where she haunts the early mornings with her clacking keyboard. Follow her on Twitter via @HaileyPiperSays or visit her website at www.haileypiper.com.

MARISSA JAMES

Marissa James writes, works and occasionally naps in the Portland area. She has had work published by a number of venues including *Daily Science Fiction*, *Third Flatiron Press* and *tdotSpec* and forthcoming from *Hybrid Ink Press*. You can find more from her on Twitter (@marofthebooks).

KURT NEWTON

Kurt Newton's stories have appeared in numerous magazines and anthologies over the years, including *Dream of Shadows*, *Weird Tales*, *Dark Discoveries*, *Weirdbook* and *Hinnom Magazine*. He is the author of two novels, *The Wishnik* and *Powerlines*. He lives in Connecticut.

You can find more of his work on his Amazon author page at https://www.amazon.com/Kurt-Newton/e/B006VYUMUM.

MORGAN ELEKTRA

Born in Woodstock, NY, Morgan Elektra discovered her passion for writing at a young age, penning stories of monsters at the dining room table. She currently lives near Savannah, Georgia with her husband, their cat Harlequin and – if the rumours are to be believed (and she sincerely hopes they are) – an awful lot of ghosts. Her work has been featured in *Gothic Fantasy: Supernatural Short Stories* and *Myths, Moons, and Mayhem*, an erotic gay menage collection. She has previously published *A Single Heartbeat*, *A Kiss of Brimstone* and *Protecting His Pack* with MLR Press.

You can find more on her website at https://bymorganelektra.wordpress.com/.

STEVEN ROOKE

Steven Rooke was born in the wilds of Essex following divine intervention. Emerging from the bush as a buff, bronzed demigod, he set out to battle mighty monsters, rescue beautiful princesses and save fabulous kingdoms. Finding Essex bereft of mighty monsters, the princesses pretty average-looking and the kingdoms less than fabulous, he decided instead to have a beer. When he'd finished crying into it, he set out for the even wilder wilds of Newcastle-Upon-Tyne to study an English degree. After three years of slogging through literature's greats, Steven realised that he could write far better than any of that bunch of talentless clowns. And so he has.

Dear Reader,

Thank you very much for supporting Dream of Shadows by buying a copy of our second issue. We hope you enjoyed our collection. Don't forget that you can still buy Issue 1 on Amazon.

We would appreciate it if you could leave us a friendly review on Amazon and spread the word.

You can also visit our website (www.dreamofshadows.co.uk) and follow us on Facebook (@dreamofshadows) to read our monthly stories.

Filipe Lichtenheld
Editor

Printed in Great Britain
by Amazon